Crash!

The sound of a huge rock bounding down the side of the Rip somewhere up ahead yanked Jake out of his worried thoughts. Then, with a roar and a clatter, more stones fell. He grinned. Nog was outdoing himself up on the cliffs.

Jake heard shouts of alarm coming from the Turnaway camp, and he set off at a trot, bending low and trying to keep boulders between him and any watchers. As he got closer to the entrance to the camp, he could hear the Turnaways shouting.

"Another fall! Get away from the cliff!"

"We need help over here, quick! One of the huts is blocked!"

A metal drawbridge lay across the central drainage channel, but fortunately the guards had not drawn it up. Even better, it was unguarded, the Turnaways having run off to help rescue others trapped in the rockslide. Jake hurried across the bridge . . . and blundered right into a group of rebels carrying shovels and pickaxes. . . .

Star Trek: The Next Generation

Starfleet Academy

#1 Worf's First Adventure
#2 Line of Fire
#3 Survival

Star Trek: Deep Space Nine

#1 The Star Ghost
#2 Stowaways

Available from MINSTREL Books

For orders other than by individual consumers, Minstrel Books grants a discount on the purchase of **10 or more** copies of single titles for special markets or premium use. For further details, please write to the Vice-President of Special Markets, Pocket Books, 1230 Avenue of the Americas, New York, NY 10020.

For information on how individual consumers can place orders, please write to Mail Order Department, Paramount Publishing, 200 Old Tappan Road, Old Tappan, NJ 07675.

STOWAWAYS

BRAD STRICKLAND

Interior illustrations by
Todd Cameron Hamilton

PUBLISHED BY POCKET BOOKS

New York London Toronto Sydney Tokyo Singapore

This book is a work of fiction. Names, characters, places, and incidents either are products of the author's imagination or are used fictitiously. Any resemblance to actual events or locales or persons, living or dead, is entirely coincidental.

A MINSTREL PAPERBACK *ORIGINAL*

A Minstrel Book published by
POCKET BOOKS, a division of Simon & Schuster Inc.
1230 Avenue of the Americas, New York, NY 10020

This book is published by Pocket Books, a division of Simon & Schuster Inc., under exclusive license from Paramount Pictures.

ISBN: 0-671-88000-4

First Minstrel Books printing April 1994

10 9 8 7 6 5 4 3 2 1

Cover art by Alan Gutierrez

Printed in the U.S.A.

This one's for Jonathan,
and he knows why.

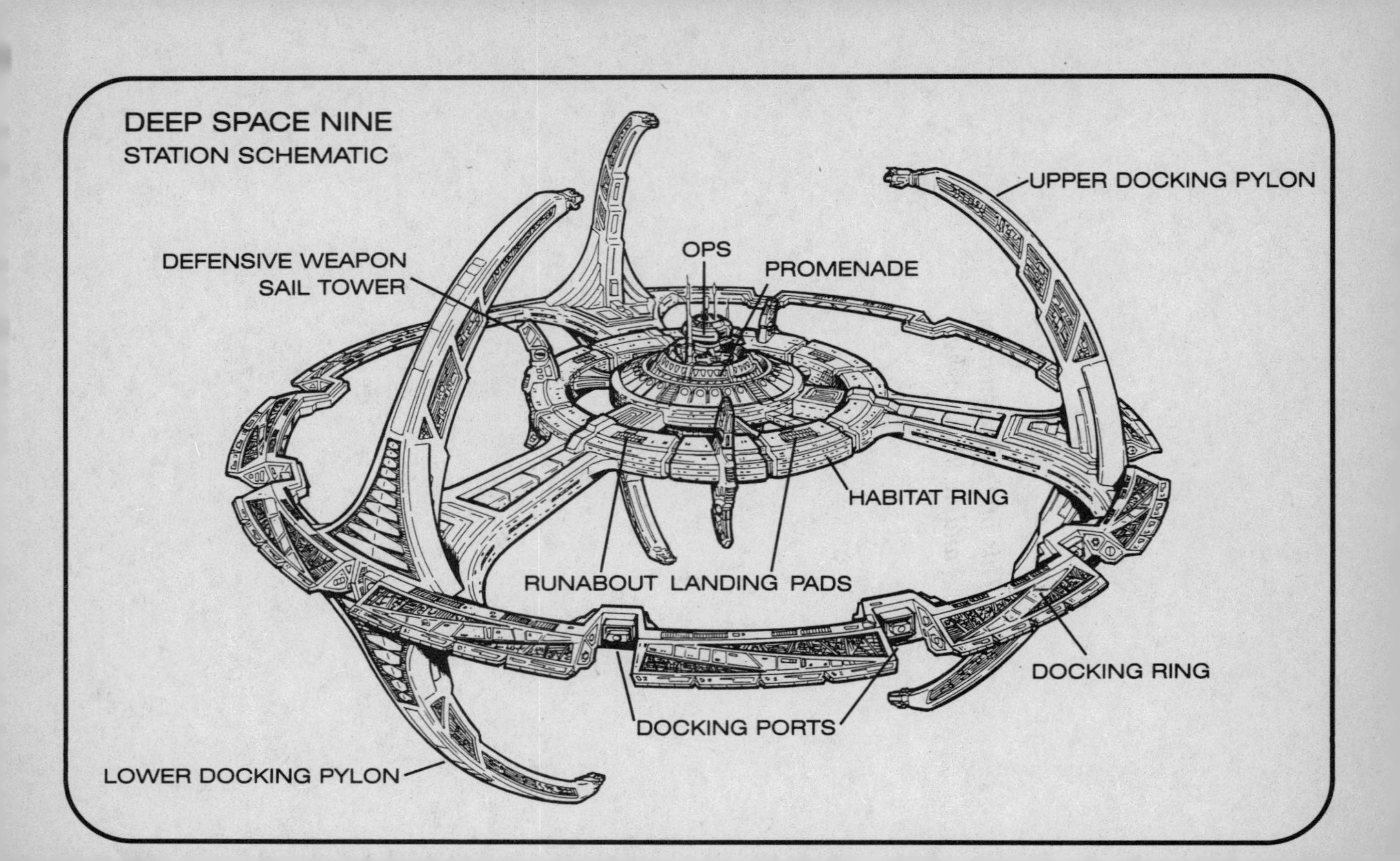
DEEP SPACE NINE
STATION SCHEMATIC
UPPER DOCKING PYLON
DEFENSIVE WEAPON
SAIL TOWER
OPS
PROMENADE
HABITAT RING
RUNABOUT LANDING PADS
DOCKING RING
DOCKING PORTS
LOWER DOCKING PYLON

STAR TREK®: DEEP SPACE NINE™

Cast of Characters

JAKE SISKO—Jake is a young teenager and the only human boy permanently on board Deep Space Nine. Jake's mother died when he was very young. He came to the space station with his father but found very few kids his own age. He doesn't remember life on Earth, but he loves baseball and candy bars, and he hates homework. His father doesn't approve of his friendship with Nog.

NOG—He is a Ferengi boy whose primary goal in life—like all Ferengi—is to make money. His father, Rom, is frequently away on business, which is fine with Nog. His uncle, Quark, keeps an eye on him. Nog thinks humans are odd with their notions of trust and favors and friendship. He doesn't always understand Jake, but since his father forbids him to hang out with the human boy, Nog and Jake are best friends. Nog loves to play tricks on people, but he tries to avoid Odo whenever possible.

COMMANDER BENJAMIN SISKO—Jake's father has been appointed by Starfleet Command to oversee the operations of the space station and act as a liaison between the Federation and Bajor. His wife was killed in a Borg attack, and he is raising Jake by himself. He is a very busy man who always tries to make time for his son.

ODO—The security officer was found by Bajoran scientists years ago, but Odo has no idea where he originally came from. He is a shape-shifter, and thus can assume any shape for a period of time. He normally maintains a vaguely human appearance but every sixteen hours he must revert to his natural liquid state. He has no patience for lawbreakers and less for Ferengi.

MAJOR KIRA NERYS—Kira was a freedom fighter in the Bajoran underground during the Cardassian occupation of Bajor. She now represents Bajoran interests aboard the station and is Sisko's first officer. Her temper is legendary.

LIEUTENANT JADZIA DAX—An old friend of Commander Sisko's, the science officer Dax is actually two joined entities known as the Trill. There is a separate consciousness—a symbiont—in the young female host's body. Sisko knew the symbiont Dax in a previous host, which was a "he."

DR. JULIAN BASHIR—Eager for adventure, Doctor Bashir graduated at the top of his class and requested a deep-space posting. His enthusiasm sometimes gets him into trouble.

MILES O'BRIEN—Formerly the Transporter Chief aboard the *U.S.S. Enterprise,* O'Brien is now Chief of Operations on Deep Space Nine.

KEIKO O'BRIEN—Keiko was a botanist on the *Enterprise,* but she moved to the station with her husband and her young daughter, Molly. Since there is little use for her botany skills on the station, she is the teacher for all of the permanent and traveling students.

QUARK—Nog's uncle and a Ferengi businessman by trade, Quark runs his own combination restaurant/casino/holosuite venue on the Promenade, the central meeting place for much of the activity on the station. Quark has his hand in every deal on board and usually manages to stay just one step ahead of the law—usually in the shape of Odo.

STOWAWAYS

CHAPTER 1

"There," said Dr. Julian Bashir, Chief Medical Officer of Deep Space Nine. "That should feel better in a moment, Jake. How did you manage to pull a ligament, anyway?"

Wincing at the pain from his throbbing ankle, Jake Sisko began to reply, but his father, Benjamin Sisko, answered for the injured teen. "He was playing baseball." Sisko crossed his arms, looking stern and strong, just as the commanding officer of a space station should look—if only he wasn't so bossy with me, Jake thought.

"Baseball?" asked the doctor, a puzzled expression on his lean face. "What's that?"

"An old Earth game," Sisko replied before his son could answer. "Jake and I play it on the holodeck from time to time, but the unrest on Bajor has kept me so busy lately that he's been playing the game alone."

"Lots of physical activity in this game?" Bashir asked Jake.

Once again, Sisko answered: "A pitcher throws a ball, a batter tries to hit it with a wooden stick, and other players try to catch any ball that's hit. Playing baseball involves lots of running, leaping, and sliding. That's how Jake hurt his ankle—sliding into second base."

"Mm," said Dr. Bashir. "Well, I don't know what 'second base' is, exactly, but you really strained your ankle. Still hurt?"

Jake Sisko glanced at his father. The big man raised an eyebrow. "Well?" he asked his son.

"Sorry," Jake said. "I thought you were going to answer for me again, the way you always do."

Dr. Bashir laughed.

With a frown on his dark face, Sisko began, "Now, see here, young man—"

"No, don't scold him," the doctor said. "Jake's absolutely right, Commander. Parents have been doing that for ages. My father was the same way, Jake. So, just between us long-suffering sons, how is your ankle feeling now?"

Lying back on the infirmary examining table, Jake flexed his right foot. A biosynergic accelerator, a kind of fat, hollow tube, covered most of his lower leg. Lights on the instrument's control panel blinked red and yellow to show that it was radiating healing energy into his sore ankle, and moment by moment the pain was easing. "It's getting better," he said. "I can move my foot a lot more now, and my ankle isn't as stiff as it was."

"Good," Bashir said. "Another few minutes and we'll have you up and about again. You'll need to exercise the ankle carefully for the next few days, to make sure that the ligament doesn't stiffen up. I'd recommend walking for a half hour a day, but no running for the rest of the week. All right?"

"Sure," Jake said.

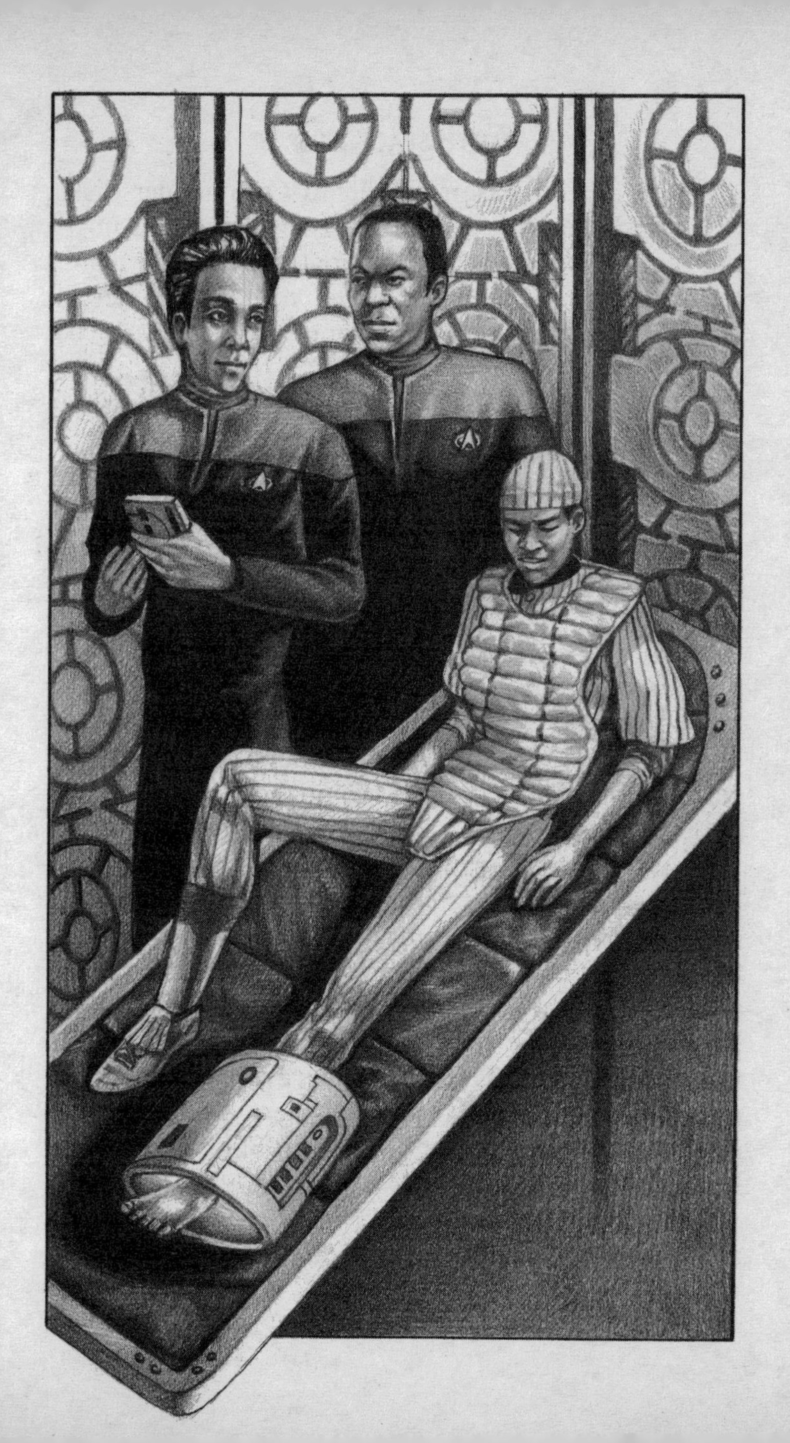

"Good man." Bashir turned to Commander Sisko. "He'll be fine. Now, as long as I have you here in my infirmary, Commander, what about giving *me* an answer to my question? While the *Excalibur* is docked here at Deep Space Nine, may I have your permission to visit Bajor?"

Sisko sighed. "Dr. Bashir, if your destination were any place other than Sakelo City—"

"But it isn't," Bashir said pleasantly. "Commander, the *Excalibur*'s medical staff is excellent, and Dr. Somak has agreed to take over my duties aboard the station for three days. I can attest to the fact that the crew of Deep Space Nine is in excellent health, thanks to my outstanding medical knowledge. Except for minor accidents, like Jake's, nothing demanding any real treatment has come up in weeks. This is a perfect time for me to visit Bajor and learn more about its people and customs, and Sakelo City is the perfect place for me to do it."

"It's a hotbed of revolt," Commander Sisko retorted. "Dr. Bashir, ever since the Cardassians left, the Bajorans have been desperately trying to pull themselves together as a people. There are factions within factions there, and civil war is just a single raid, a single assassination away. Sakelo City is the most notorious hive of rebels and revolutionaries on the planet. Why, even the Kai Opaka couldn't command full respect there while she was still on Bajor, and you know how all Bajorans honored her."

"Three days," Bashir said. "Only three days. And look at it this way, Commander—I could be a secret agent."

"A what?" asked Sisko, sounding both puzzled and amused.

The young doctor leaned forward, his expression intense. "A secret agent. I could find out the real story of the rebellious factions in Sakelo City. I've never been there, and no one there would recognize me. Lots of off-worlders land there. As you say, it's a regular den of iniquity, swarming with smugglers and shady characters. I could pretend to be an asteroid miner, or a space pirate with arms for sale. Any rebel group would get in touch with me, and I could learn all about—"

"Dr. Bashir?" asked Jake. "Uh, my ankle feels fine now." On the control panel all the lights had turned green.

The doctor coughed self-consciously and switched off the biosynergic accelerator. He opened the cylinder, and Jake pulled his foot out. "Here," said Dr. Bashir. "Let me help you down, and you can take a step or two on it to see if it will hold your weight." He put his arm around Jake and helped the fourteen-year-old slide off the examining table. When Jake stood on his own, the doctor stepped away from him. "How does that feel?"

Jake took a step, then another. "Feels great," he said with a grin. "Thanks, Doctor."

"All in the line of duty," Bashir said, returning his grin. "Now, Commander, about Bajor—"

With a rueful chuckle Sisko held up his hands. "Enough. I surrender. All right, Julian, you have my permission to visit Sakelo City for three days. On one condition, mind you."

"Condition?" asked Dr. Bashir, drawing himself up.

"Yes, sir. Anything for Starfleet. What do you want me to do, Commander?"

"Relax," said Sisko. "Relax, enjoy yourself, and don't play secret agent. Is that understood?"

Dr. Bashir looked mildly disappointed. "I suppose so," he said with a sigh.

"Very well. How soon will the *Excalibur*'s medical staff be ready to relieve you of your ordinary duties?"

"I'll need to bring all the medical summaries up to date. I'd say tomorrow, Commander."

Sisko nodded. "The runabouts are tied up, but request one of the *Excalibur* shuttlecrafts—I think the *Einstein* is free. And I'll expect you back, rested and refreshed, in three days."

"Very good, Commander," said the doctor.

Jake cleared his throat. "Uh, Dad, if Dr. Bashir doesn't mind, do you think I could go along, too?"

"That isn't a good idea," said Sisko.

"Aw, Dad," Jake complained. "You keep promising to take me down to Bajor, and you never do."

"You've been there on field trips," Sisko pointed out.

"For a couple of hours at a time," Jake said. "I want to stay on a real planet overnight, get outside, under a real sun, not just on the holodeck—"

"Dr. Bashir has made his plans," Sisko said. "I'm sure he doesn't want company."

Bashir smiled. "Well, if Jake really wants to go, I don't see why—"

"Doctor," Sisko said pleasantly but firmly, "you have made your plans, and you haven't included Jake in them. Am I right?"

"Oh," said Bashir. He swallowed. "Well, I hadn't really planned to take anyone with me, no."

"Thank you, Doctor. Come along, Jake."

Jake and his father left sickbay, with Jake fuming. "It's always like this," he complained. "You promise me that we can go to Bajor, and then something comes up on the space station and we can't do it. When we were on Mars, you kept promising me that we could visit Earth, and we never had a chance. Dad, I'm tired of living in space. I want to be on a real planet for a change, even if it's just for three days."

They stepped into a turbolift. "Ops," Sisko ordered, and the elevator car began to move. The commander sighed. "I know how much you'd like to go with Dr. Bashir, Jake. But evidently you didn't listen to what I was telling him. Sakelo City was the headquarters that the Cardassians used while stripping the southern hemisphere of the planet of its minerals. It's hardly a city, really—more a giant armed camp. It's true that the Bajorans have been trying to civilize it, to quell the rebels and the malcontents, but it's still an uncomfortable place for a human to be. Remember, the Bajorans spent forty-odd years fighting against their Cardassian overlords. A good many of them regard the Federation as little more than substitute slave-masters. Your reception in Sakelo City could be dangerous."

"But you let Dr. Bashir go—"

"Dr. Bashir is an adult," said Sisko. The turbolift stopped, and they stepped out.

Immediately a Bajoran ensign rushed up. "Commander," she said, "Major Kira says that you need to speak with the captain of the Klingon research vessel *Thuvis.* He's requesting clearance to—"

Sisko hurried away to Ops with the ensign. Jake, left behind, sighed and walked to the Promenade, the bustling, noisy commercial decks of Deep Space Nine. Jake muttered, "It just isn't fair," but no one could hear him. He caught sight of a familiar figure, short, large-headed, with huge ears, and he hurried over. "Hi, Nog," he said.

Nog, Jake's Ferengi friend, turned around with a pointy-toothed smile. "Jake! I was looking for you earlier, but Odo told me you were in the infirmary. What was wrong?"

"Oh, I hurt my foot," Jake said. "It was nothing." The two boys reached a corner where they loved to perch, legs dangling, and watch the lively panorama of the Promenade swirl by below. As they sat there, Jake told the whole story of his injury, of Dr. Bashir's planned visit to Bajor, and of his disappointment.

Nog grunted in sympathy. "I know just what you mean," he said. "This place is all right, but it's stifling. Not enough opportunity for adventure and profit. And grown-ups always around to boss you and bully you."

This time Jake made a sympathetic noise. Jake's mother was dead, and although he missed her terribly at times, he had to contend with only one protective parent. Nog had his father Rom and his uncle Quark, two Ferengi businessmen who had so far managed to keep barely inside the law as they ran a highly successful bar and restaurant on the Promenade. And both Rom and Quark never hesitated to put Nog to work or to discipline him if they thought he needed a little attention.

"I've got an idea," Nog said suddenly. "Why don't we both go to Bajor?"

"Right," Jake said. "Fat chance."

"I know a way," Nog said, his voice tempting, insinuating.

"Nog, are you crazy?" asked Jake. "My father would never give me permission to leave the station."

"Who said we asked permission?" Nog asked. His sharp-toothed grin was as ferocious as a shark's.

Jake looked at his friend with deep suspicion. "You mean sneak away? You know I can't do that."

"Oh, if you're not brave enough to go—"

Jake glowered at the Ferengi. "It isn't that. But you know Dad wouldn't like it. For one thing, it's just plain wrong. For another, I'd get killed, and so would you."

"Sure," Nog said. "But three days on a planet, with nobody to boss us around, nobody to put us to work, nobody to punish us. Three days to do anything we wanted to do. Three whole days to be as free as a Ferengi crocohippus—now, wouldn't that be worth getting killed a little?"

"Maybe," Jake said doubtfully. He thought of how tired he was of Deep Space Nine and of how great it would feel to be out in the open, under a real sky. He even had a break from school now, because it was one of the vacation breaks. Still, he knew he would feel terribly guilty about disobeying his father. Of course, he thought, if his father didn't actually *tell* him not to go to Bajor, he wouldn't exactly be disobeying him. After all, Jake's dad

had not forbidden his son to go. He had only said it wasn't a good idea, which was a different matter altogether.

As if he knew what Jake was thinking, Nog slyly added, "Your dad might not even find out about it, if we're smart. I think my father and my uncle may help us there."

It was an extremely tempting offer for someone as tired of staying on a space station as Jake was. He wavered, an uncertain grin starting to spread across his face. "Tell me more."

As they sat above the Promenade, swinging their legs

and enjoying their privacy, Nog whispered a daring and shady plan. A plan that would indeed call for punishment from their fathers. A plan that would, no doubt, get them in deep trouble.

And before long Jake was laughing and nodding his head in complete agreement.

CHAPTER 2

Jake sat quietly in the restaurant section of Quark's place, eating a hot-fudge sundae and wishing he had ears the size of Nog's. That would let him eavesdrop a lot better on the conversation that Nog was having with his uncle Quark. "Lots of off-world travelers in Sakelo City, Uncle," Nog was saying slyly. "I imagine that some of them will have interesting knickknacks for sale cheap. If I had a few of those to resell here on Deep Space Nine, I could make a handsome profit."

Quark was busy mixing some complicated drink for a poker-faced Vulcan. "Mm-hmm," he said absently. "I like the way you think, Nog. But Sakelo City is strictly off-limits, so you can forget it." He delivered the drink to the Vulcan with a flourish. "Here you are," Quark said to the customer. "A delicious, cool, hundred-fruit cooler."

"Nonalcoholic," the Vulcan said.

"Absolutely!" exclaimed Quark. "I know Vulcan preferences."

The Vulcan picked up the tall glass, swirled it so that the multicolored juices inside made rainbow spirals of yellow, red, orange, green, blue, and violet. He sipped it carefully, then raised one slanted eyebrow in appreciation. "This is very acceptable," he murmured.

Quark beamed. "Thank you, sir. And I hope you will remember to mention to all your friends that Quark specializes in all sorts of vegetarian and fruit delights." The Ferengi gave the bar and restaurant a quick, all-encompassing glance, moved down the bar, and beckoned Nog to follow him. Now they were a little closer to Jake, and he strained his ears to hear Quark's confidential whisper: "I've been thinking it over, Nephew. You have a good point about Sakelo City. But the difficulty remains: How would you get there?"

"There is a way, Uncle," said Nog. In a few words he explained that Dr. Bashir had special permission to visit Sakelo City and would be going there tomorrow. "So," Nog finished, "all I have to do is find some way to stow away on the *Einstein.* Then I could spend three days in the Sakelo bazaar, picking up anything I could, and I'd bring it all back here to sell for a profit."

"But you'd be sure to be detected," Quark said.

"Yes, Uncle. That is why I need your help—and Father's, too."

"Ah," responded Quark. "Now we come to it."

"You have great skills in overriding computer systems," Nog said. "If you could just arrange a blind spot, maybe in one of the storage compartments, so the computer could not detect an extra passenger, then we could succeed."

With a wolfish grin Quark said, "That would be easy enough. And what is in it for me, Nephew?"

Nog squawked in protest. Jake took another big bite of hot-fudge sundae and smiled to himself. He tuned out the inevitable round of Ferengi bargaining that came next, but he did notice with satisfaction when Quark hissed between his teeth and said, "Very well! It is a bargain—but only because you are my brother's son and I have a soft spot for you. All I can say is that the trip had better be very profitable."

Jake finished the last of his sundae, got up, and strolled away. A grinning Nog caught up with him not far from Quark's place. "I did it!" he said. "My uncle will adjust the computer, and no one will be able to tell that we're aboard the *Einstein.* And Uncle Quark will persuade my father to cover for you. Best of all, it will only cost half my profits. Now there is just one problem left."

"What's that?" Jake asked.

"I don't have much money," Nog admitted. "So I won't be able to trade for much in the way of goods. Do you, uh, happen to know where I might, ah, borrow—"

Jake laughed. "I've got some credits saved up in my allowance account," he said. "You can borrow them. Just pay me back after you and Quark have finished all your business."

"Fine," said Nog. He gave Jake a shrewd glance. "Now, as to the matter of the interest you will charge me, I won't pay a credit over—"

"Forget the interest," Jake said. "Just give me back the amount of the loan, that's all."

Shaking his huge, bald head, Nog murmured, "Earth people. They're all crazy."

That evening Jake had even more good news. His father told him that the Federation was sending a few members of the *Excalibur*'s crew to Vigan Delta Five, a planet in a system not too far from the Bajoran system. The Starfleet crew were on a diplomatic mission, paying a courtesy call to the natives of Vigan Delta Five, and Commander Sisko was personally piloting the runabout that would take them there and back. "So you'll have to do without me for a few days," Sisko finished. With an odd expression he said, "Rom tells me you're welcome to spend the time with Nog in their quarters. He says he wants to offer us a gesture of friendship. Is that all right with you?"

"Sure, Dad," Jake said, trying hard not to grin. "Uh, how long will you be gone?"

"Yes, well, watch yourself," Sisko said. "I've rarely known a Ferengi to offer anything out of the goodness of his heart—"

"It'll be fine, Dad. Nog is my friend," replied Jake.

"Well—behave yourself, then. Now, the Vigan Delta system is about one day's journey from here," Sisko said. "The diplomatic mission will take perhaps two days. So we should be back on Deep Space Nine in four or five days."

"All right," Jake said, though inside he was positively gloating. Four or five days! He and Nog would be back from Bajor before his father returned to Deep Space Nine. With a little luck, Jake thought, Sisko would never even find out that he had been gone. Things were working out perfectly.

Jake sneaked away right after breakfast the next morning. Carrying a small valise with a couple of changes of clothing and his allowance inside, he made his way to the docking ring section of Deep Space Nine as inconspicuously as possible. He met Nog, who carried a well-stuffed backpack. No one paid any attention to the two, possibly because they were such a familiar sight. Both of them loved to hang around the docking ring and spot the exotic travelers coming in from the far reaches of the quadrant.

Nog led the way to the airlock connecting to the *Einstein*'s docking port. He touched the controls, and the great geared hatch-cover rolled away. Nog glanced around, but no one was watching. "Hurry," he said. "My uncle has temporarily disabled the security detectors in this corridor. They'll come on line again just as soon as the hatch closes behind us."

The two hustled through the airlock. The hatch closed behind them. "Pretty smart," Jake said admiringly. "Chief O'Brien will think it's just another Cardassian computer malfunction."

Nog giggled and nodded. Chief of Operations O'Brien had strong opinions on the value of Cardassian engineering systems, and they were all scornful. Nog tapped a control panel beside an interior hatch, and it hissed open, revealing a closet-size space. "In here," he said.

The two friends ducked inside, and Nog closed the hatch. The light stayed on, since the local sensors recognized their presence in the compartment—even though Quark had made sure the sensors did not report them to the shuttle computer. "Isn't this a storage compartment for space suits?" Jake whispered.

"Right," Nog answered. "Emergency suits, in case the shuttle loses pressurization. But there's another compartment right across from us, and there are five suits in there. Since there are only three of us along on this trip, we're safe enough."

"I didn't mean that," Jake said. "I was just wondering what happened to the space suits that were in here."

"My uncle's taking care of them," Nog said.

Jake felt a qualm. If Quark were taking care of the space suits, chances were the Federation would never see its property again. He had no time to speak to Nog about his doubts, though. Jake heard the faint sound of the airlock opening and closing, and then the hiss of the *Einstein*'s main hatch as someone entered. After another moment he could hear Dr. Bashir's voice: "Ops, this is the shuttle *Einstein,* ready for departure."

After a brief delay someone in Ops replied, *"Einstein,* you are clear for departure. Enjoy your holiday, Doctor."

Jake blinked as he heard Bashir's confident reply: "It isn't exactly a holiday. But thanks for the good wishes. I'm off."

The shuttle shivered as the docking clamps released their hold. Then the thrusters came to life, and Jake had a momentary sense of movement as the *Einstein*'s inertia-damping field took over the gravity from Deep Space Nine. Then the engines settled into a powerful roar, and the ship was in flight.

"How long to Bajor?" Nog whispered.

"Couple of hours," Jake replied. "Not long."

"Did you bring anything to eat?" the Ferengi asked.

Jake smiled and dug into his valise. "Couple of chocolate bars," he said, offering one to Nog.

Nog made a face. "Yuck!" he exclaimed. "How can you stand that stuff? Don't you have any glop, or maybe some crystal tinglers?"

"Sorry," Jake said. "It's chocolate or nothing."

With an exaggerated sigh Nog said, "Hand it over, then. I'll try to learn to like it."

"Take off the wrapper this time," suggested Jake. "That way it won't be quite as chewy."

"The paper is the best part," Nog growled, though quietly.

For a few seconds they both munched their chocolate bars. Then, suddenly, they both stiffened as they heard Bashir's voice. It rang out loudly, with an edge of sharp command: "Counterespionage Control, this is Secret Agent Bashir, heading for Sakelo City. I intend to clean out that vile den. Any special instructions?"

Nog's eyes were wide with shock and surprise. "What does he mean by that?" he demanded in a startled whisper.

Jake could only shake his head. He had no idea whom Bashir was calling, or what his strange message meant. Jake held a finger to his lips and listened hard.

"Yes, Control, I can do that," Bashir said. "It's all in a day's work for a top-notch secret agent like yours truly. What? Please repeat that—and don't worry, I'm on the prime security subspace channel, with the scrambler on full confusion."

Though he tried as hard as he could, Jake could hear

no one except the doctor. From the baffled look on Nog's face, Jake guessed that the Ferengi boy, even with his vast and sensitive ear equipment, could hear only the doctor, too. At that moment Bashir laughed scornfully. "Of course I know it's dangerous, man! But danger means nothing to me. I'll be back in three days with the news that the rebel conspiracy has been smashed, or my name isn't Julian Bashir, the Space Falcon!"

Jake started to giggle. Desperately he covered his laughter so that it came out as short wheezes and gasps. Nog looked at him as if he had suddenly gone out of his mind. "What is it?" persisted Nog. "Who is he talking to?"

"No-nobody," Jake gasped. "He—he's just playing."

"Playing? He's an adult!" Nog objected.

Jake shrugged. "Still. He's pretending to be a great spy known as the Space Falcon. He's not on the subspace radio at all. He's just pretending to talk to his headquarters. It's a game, except he's using his imagination, not the holodeck."

With a disgusted look Nog snorted, "Humans!" He popped the last of his chocolate bar into his mouth and ate it without even bothering to complain about the taste.

Several more times during the trip, Dr. Bashir pretended to speak to counterespionage control, whatever that was. He asked for any clues that other, less gifted, spies had discovered, requested an update on the Bajoran political situation, and discussed the various factions of the Bajoran government with his imaginary secret-agent friends. Nog soon ignored all this and dropped off into a light sleep, sitting on the storage

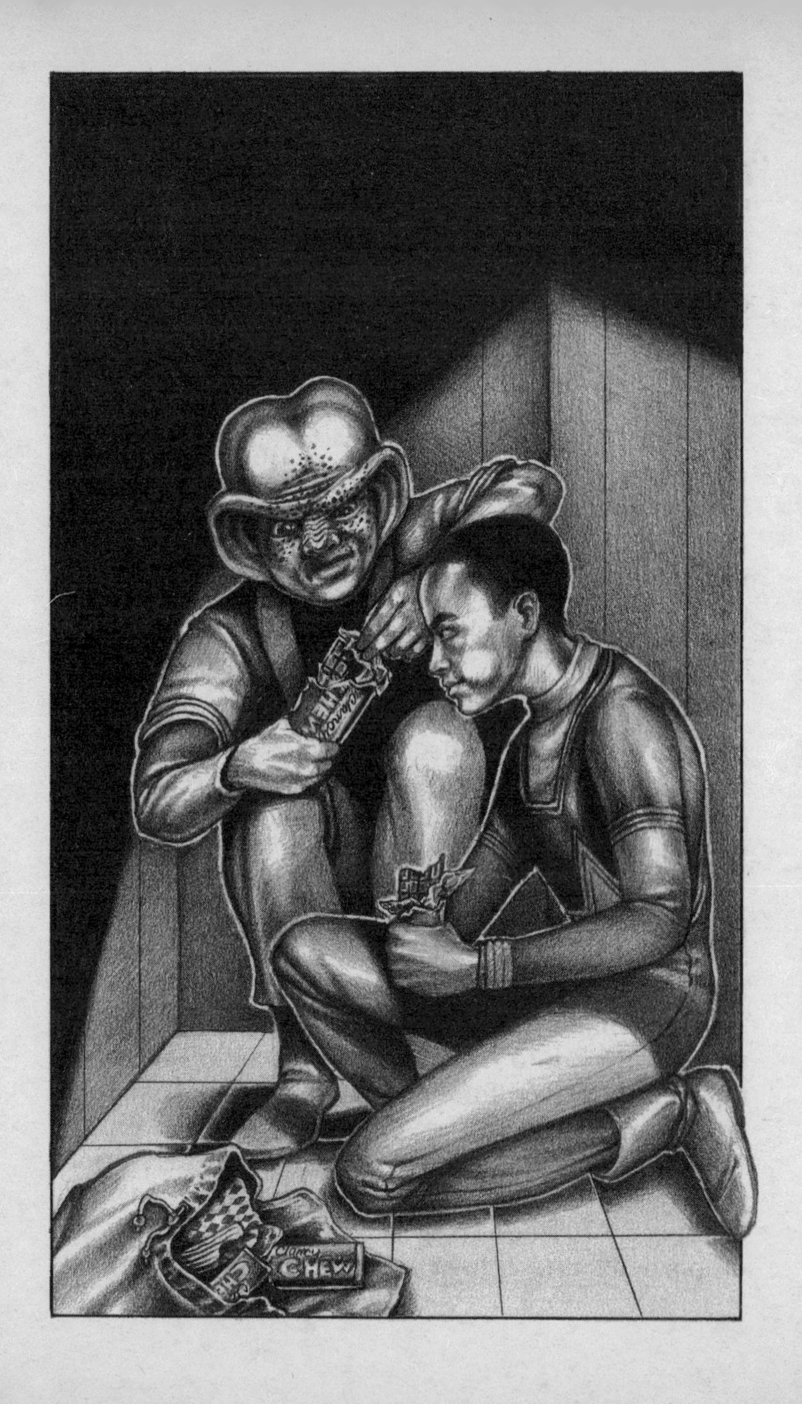
Clancy
CHEW

compartment floor and hugging his knees, his large head lolling to one side. Jake sat opposite him. It was a tight fit. Their toes touched each other. Jake wished he could doze, too, because he had been so excited about the trip to Bajor that he had hardly slept the night before. He still was too keyed up to sleep, and so he listened to Dr. Bashir's imaginary transmissions, grinned at their wildness, and tried not to laugh.

Eventually Dr. Bashir spoke to someone who actually spoke back. He asked for clearance to land at the Sakelo Hub spaceport, and after a moment or two a Bajoran voice said, "Permission granted, shuttle *Einstein.* You will land on East Pad Seven. Is your shuttlecraft standard Federation design?"

"Yes, it is," Bashir responded.

"Very well. Prepare to transfer control to us in thirty standard seconds from . . . *now.*"

Half a minute passed, with the Bajoran controller counting down the last fifteen seconds. Then the roar of the engines changed pitch, and Jake felt a slight change in gravity. The shuttle's inertial damping had been turned off, and now Bajor's gravity, slightly less than Earth normal, was taking the place of the artificial gravity. The ship settled in with a few light bumps, and then the controller said, "Welcome to Bajor, shuttle *Einstein.* Please wait for your escort outside your craft. Your escort will arrange for any routine maintenance your craft may need and will process you through a brief welcoming protocol."

"Do I have to go through customs?" asked Bashir.

"Customs?" asked the controller, sounding surprised. "No, of course not. We have a treaty with the Federation.

You are free to come and go as you choose. It's just a formality, to make sure you can find your way around the city."

"I see." The doctor's voice took on some of its make-believe edge: "Then this is Dr. Julian Bashir, reporting to Sakelo City, Planet Bajor."

"Er—of course," said the Bajoran controller.

Jake heard the doctor walk past their hiding place, and then he heard the shuttle door open and close. After a few seconds more, when he was sure that the doctor had left the ship, he nudged Nog's foot. "Wake up!" he said. "We're here!"

"Um?" Nog asked, stirring and stretching. "We landed?"

"About five minutes ago," Jake said.

"Hmm. I didn't even notice. Dr. Bashir is a better pilot than I thought," Nog said. "Is the beach transparent?"

"Huh?" asked Jake.

Nog looked irritated. "I thought that was an old Earth expression," he said. "It means 'Is anyone looking?'"

Shaking his head, Jake said, "You got it a little wrong. The expression should be, 'Is the coast clear?' And the answer is, I don't know. Let's take a look." Quietly the two boys rose. Nog opened the storage hatch, and they stepped out into the empty shuttle. They paused at the shuttle door while Jake peered out through the viewports. "Nobody is looking," he said. "Let's go!"

Nog opened the shuttle door, and they stepped out onto a raised circular platform. It was one of a cluster of nine, and one of the few that was occupied. Three of the others had small craft on them: a personal space yacht (though it looked a little old and beaten-up), a spherical Mendebelan personal transport, and a shiny asteroid hopper. No one was around any of them.

It was early morning in this part of Bajor, with a clear sky and bright sunlight. After a bit of exploring, Nog found a stair that wound around the side of the cylindrical landing pad, and then they hurried through a long, dim tunnel. Light shone at the far end. They came out into a sunny plaza, its pale orange brick walkways crowded with people from dozens of planets, all of them apparently talking, laughing, and cursing at the top of their lungs. Humble shops lined the walks, their small windows hopefully displaying goods for sale. Many more merchants did business in the open air, from carts or even from the vast pockets of their robes. A juggler in gaudy red, green, and yellow silks danced through the crowd while keeping three flaming torches spinning in the air, trailing streamers of blue smoke. A pretty, dark-haired Bajoran girl laughed and clapped her hands, her brass bracelets jangling. A procession of hooded Bajoran priests came by, mumbling a string of blessings to passersby. A plump merchant respectfully saluted the priests with one hand while he jingled a heavy purse in the other. Jake and Nog hung back a little, for ahead of them in the crowd they could see Dr. Bashir taking it all in as he sauntered along.

Strange sights, smells, and sounds washed over them. "Man," Jake said. "This is gonna be great."

"I agree," Nog said. He stood with his head jerking from side to side. To the left was the pretty girl, and on the right was the merchant's fat purse. Nog was obviously attracted by both. "So little time"—he sighed—"so much opportunity." He clapped Jake on the back. "Stick with me," he said, "and I'll make you the happiest human on Bajor—except, of course, for the Space Falcon!" The crowd parted and stared at the two young men as they walked together, laughing like Rigellian howling hodo birds.

CHAPTER 3

The Space Falcon apparently was hungry. He had wandered through some dark, twisting back streets, waving away merchants and peddlers, until he came out into another plaza, this one a clutter of tables and chairs outside a domed Bajoran restaurant. A pretty Bajoran serving woman came smiling up to him and asked if he cared to eat. "Yes," Dr. Bashir said, returning her smile. "If you can give me an inconspicuous table, one where I will not be noticed."

The server looked a little puzzled at that, but she nodded agreeably and led Dr. Bashir to a small oval table with two chairs. Then she recited the menu. The doctor ordered sevala, a sort of local pasta, and a mesto salad of local vegetables, along with mineral water. The server nodded and hurried away, and the doctor leaned back, his eyes narrowing as he scanned the other patrons of the restaurant.

"He's checking for enemies of the Federation," Nog whispered.

Jake had to clamp his mouth shut to keep from laughing. The two boys had caught sight of the doctor in the crowd and had followed him here with absolutely no difficulty. Now they shared a table across the plaza from Bashir, safely screened from him by a bushy, sharp-leafed plant. Nog was in high spirits, for already he had bought some rings carved from the shell of a native mollusk and had traded these for some intricate copper bracelets, quite valuable on a planet stripped of most of its metal ores. He was sure he would be able to trade the bracelets for something even more valuable. So far he had spent almost nothing, and already he anticipated huge profits. He would be in his father's and uncle's good graces for a month.

As for Jake, he was getting a little impatient. He lacked Nog's Ferengi enthusiasm for bargaining and trading, and he wanted to see more of Sakelo City. Still, Nog had suggested that it would be good to discover where the doctor would be staying, and Jake realized that he was right. So they took their places at the table and ordered drinks—redfruit juice for Jake, and a nauseating concoction called a Bajoran fizz for Nog. As they sipped them, they kept the doctor under close observation, and he never once noticed that they were nearby.

"What is he doing now?" Nog asked as Dr. Bashir finished his meal.

Jake had to lean forward a little to see through the fronds of the plant. "It looks like he's talking to his sleeve," he said. Then he laughed. "He's pretending to have a secret subspace radio built into his cuff. He's

probably reporting on the meal to counterespionage control right now."

"Wait a minute," Nog said. "Who's this?"

Jake frowned. A poorly dressed Bajoran had sidled up to Dr. Bashir and had bowed deeply to him. The doctor looked flustered and startled, but after a moment he nodded and indicated the other chair. The deeply tanned Bajoran man, with an anxious glance around, settled into it and leaned across the table. The two were soon speaking rapidly to each other, but their voices were too low for Jake to hear.

Nog, however, had no trouble at all. His large ears were supersensitive, and he kept up a commentary on the action. "This fellow says his name is Tikar Antol," Nog reported. "Now he's asking Dr. Bashir if he's a Starfleet officer. Dr. Bashir is saying he knows some officers. Tikar says he has some information that might be very valuable to the Federation. Now Dr. Bashir wants to know what it is. Tikar won't say. He thinks it would be better to show the doctor than to tell him. He's asking what the doctor's name is. Dr. Bashir says his name is Cosmo Peregrine. What in the world does that mean?"

With a chuckle Jake said, "Cosmo comes from an old Earth word meaning 'space,' and a peregrine is a kind of falcon. He's making believe again."

"Shhh," Nog said. "Now Mr. Tikar says he has a landtran nearby and that they can go to see this big secret. Dr. Bashir is calling the server over to pay his bill. I guess he's going to go with the Bajoran. Yes, there they go! Quick, can you settle up here?"

Heaving a sigh, Jake left a Bajoran one-credit token on the table. It was the smallest he had, but it was easily four times too much to pay for a couple of drinks. But Nog was already hurrying away after the retreating Dr. Bashir, and Jake had to hustle to catch up.

In and out of colonnades, narrow streets, and open plazas went Bashir, side by side with Tikar Antol. At last they came to an open street dominated by a huge ruined building. Jake took a deep breath. The ruin was not in the normal Bajoran style, for a good reason. The Cardassians had built it. Once it must have stood as a glowering dark fortress; now it was a hollow shell. No doubt the Bajorans had torn the building apart as soon as the hated Cardassians had left the planet. Whatever it had been, administration center, warehouse, or prison, it was just a wreck now.

But the other side of the street was a row of simple Bajoran domed shops. Parked along this side was a strange assortment of vehicles, from sun-powered three-wheeled electrocars to rickety wooden-wheeled farm carts drawn by muscular horned animals with wrinkled green hides. Tikar and Bashir stepped into a landtran, a rectangular open car with caterpillar treads instead of wheels. This one was sand-colored, old, and very battered, splotched all over with rust. For a moment Bashir sat there with an uncertain expression, as if he were not quite sure about this clunky vehicle and his expedition in it. Then, to Jake's surprise, the old-fashioned alcohol combustion engine coughed to life right away, and the landtran moved out onto the dusty street. Dr. Bashir grasped the side as the car went jouncing and bouncing along, kicking up a cloud of yellow dust behind it.

"Lost him!" Nog said. "Well, any suggestions now?"

Jake thought. Bajorans were a spiritual people, or at least they had been before the Cardassians conquered their planet and enslaved them. Still, a lot of the old religious traditions still existed. "I know where we can pick up his trail again. I'll bet he was going to stay in the Hospitality Tower," Jake said at last.

"The what?" asked Nog, who was no student of Bajoran folkways.

"It's sort of a hotel," Jake explained. "The monks of the Order of Hispin run them in most of Bajor's cities. Travelers can get a room for the night for free."

"For free?" asked Nog. He shook his large bald head. "Bajorans are just as crazy as humans," he moaned. Then he brightened. "But if they give away rooms for free, let's go there ourselves. That will save our money for more important transactions."

They asked for directions. Sure enough, Sakelo City had a Hospitality Tower, and before long they found it. A small garden was out front, and a half-dozen Bajoran monks wearing plain tan hooded robes worked there, watering and weeding. One of them led the two boys to the Keeper of Keys, a silver-haired Bajoran monk with a glint of good humor in his gray eyes. "So," the man said, "you two are travelers, eh?"

"Yes, sir," said Jake.

"I don't suppose you are here for the elevation of the Vedek," the monk said.

Jake blinked. "Uh—the what?"

With a smile the monk said, "One of the chief leaders of our religion is called Vedek. The new Vedek is to take the position the day after tomorrow. A festival will celebrate Carik Madal's new eminence."

"Is Carik Madal the new—Vedek?" asked Jake.

"He is. It is the first time in my life that a man has been elected to the position instead of a woman. Many do not think that a good omen, but Carik is a gentle man who has, nevertheless, a strong will. He will be a good voice to have speaking for us on the Vedek Assembly. But you boys care little for our local affairs. How long will you stay?"

Jake said, "We'll be here for three days. Do you have a room we could use?"

"You are fortunate, because as it happens, we do, even

with the crowds of the festival coming into the city," said the Keeper. He tilted his head. "You are human, are you not?" he asked Jake.

"Yes, sir, I am," Jake replied. "My friend is a Ferengi."

The Keeper inclined his head. "May you find good trading," he said to Nog.

A surprised Nog murmured his thanks.

Jake said, "Uh, I think another human may come here later. Dr. Julian Bashir, from the Deep Space Nine station."

"Ah, yes," said the Keeper. "He called from the station yesterday to make sure a room would be available. Are you boys friends of his?"

"Yes," Jake said. "We'd like to surprise him. Could you sort of tell us where he will be, and then not tell him that we are here?"

"If he asks, I must tell the truth."

"Oh, sure," Jake said. "If he asks. But if he doesn't—"

"Then you may surprise him."

Jake relaxed. Dr. Bashir had no idea that he and Nog had stowed away aboard the *Einstein.* It was very unlikely that he would casually ask the monks if any other humans were at the Hospitality Tower.

They learned that Dr. Bashir was staying in the Meditation Wing, Fireflower Room. Their own room would be in the same wing, but two floors higher, the Spiral Shell Room. They accepted the old-fashioned key and found their way to the room, which proved to be light and airy, with two windows looking out over another commercial plaza and the monks' garden. Two simple beds, a table, and two chairs were all the furniture. The room also had a small closet and an adjoining bathroom.

Nog tossed his backpack onto one of the beds. "I'm off," he announced. "There are profits to be made, and a time of festival can double them. Are you coming?"

Jake left his valise on the other bed. "Lead on," he said. "We'll pick up the Space Falcon's trail here this evening, or maybe tomorrow morning."

Sakelo City turned out to be a warren of different neighborhoods, some squalid and poor with tumble-down buildings and wretched-looking people, others rich and plush. As the afternoon moved on toward sunset and twilight, the press of people in the many open bazaars grew thicker and thicker. Nog and Jake saw a native aspth charmer—aspths were reptilian, something like red and black striped snakes but with hundreds of small legs. Their heads were long and triangular, with jet-black saber fangs that flashed in the light. Evidently they were poisonous, because when one of them made a sudden movement, the crowd watching fell away with gasps of alarm. The charmer, though, would distract the animals with waves of his hands and low, musical chantings. He wore only full scarlet trousers. His chest and arms were deeply tanned but absolutely bare and glistening with sweat. His deadly creatures would rear the forward third of their bodies up, swaying and staring at their master with cold red eyes, and occasionally they would lunge, but he always pulled his hand away at the last instant, and he was never bitten.

In the next plaza were street magicians in billowing green robes who made bear-size "rabbits" disappear, and contortionists who could tie their arms and legs in knots, and acrobats who leapt and tumbled with astonishing grace. Fire jugglers made arcs and rainbows of different-colored flaming balls, never holding them in their hands long enough to be burned. Toothless old men and women in the black and white robes of soothsayers came cackling toward the boys offering to foretell their future, and there were beautiful dancing girls who wore bracelets on their wrists and ankles of tiny silver and coral bells, so that they danced to the notes of a sweet, wild music they made themselves.

And of course there were businesspeople selling all sorts of things: glowsilk kerchiefs, native gemstones, polished rocks with weird fossils visible in them, delicate and intricate jewelry made of bronze, copper, and even the exceedingly rare metals like silver and gold. Nog made a dozen deals, and he looked more pleased after each one. Finally the sun sank low. Torches began to flare in the streets, and many of the merchants' booths folded down into themselves as the business day ended. Jake and Nog ate dinner at another Bajoran restaurant, and then they made their way back to the Hospitality Tower. The Keeper of Keys told them that their friend had not yet appeared, so they went up to their own room.

Nog spread out his purchases on the table and gloated over them, but Jake stood at the window looking down into the darkened plaza. "I'm worried," he said. "What do you suppose has happened to Dr. Bashir?"

"Oh, he's all right," Nog said with confidence. "He's off being told some outrageous lies by that trickster Tikar, and he's enjoying every minute of it. Sometime late tonight, Tikar will tell the good doctor that he will give him the secret password used by the Bajoran rebels for only fifty credits. Dr. Bashir will bargain as shrewdly as an Earth person ever does and in the end will pay fifty credits. Tikar will give him some nonsense word, and then the Space Falcon will return to his nest for the night, satisfied that he has saved the galaxy."

"It's been hours," Jake said.

"That's the way it always works," responded Nog. "Jake, the way a confidence man operates is like that. The longer the time you take to build up the victim, the bigger the payoff you can expect."

Jake came over to the table and sat across from Nog. "I suppose there is a Rule of Acquisition that covers such things," he said. All Ferengi memorized the Rules of Acquisition at an early age. They were like sacred writings to the merchant race.

"Of course," agreed Nog. " 'The more time they take deciding, the more money they will spend.' It's an elementary principle."

"I wish he would come back," Jake said.

The boys got ready for bed not long after that. Nog fell asleep at once and soon was snoring away contentedly, but Jake could not sleep. He kept remembering how seedy and untrustworthy the Bajoran had looked as he sidled up to Dr. Bashir in the restaurant. Lying in the quiet darkness, Jake worried about Dr. Bashir. He hoped that Nog was right, and that the doctor was just indulging his love of playacting. He hoped that Tikar Antol was just a harmless con artist—or at least that he intended only financial harm. He hoped that, wherever Dr. Bashir was, he was safe and sound.

But somehow he knew in his heart that this was not the case.

Something told him that Dr. Bashir was in trouble. That he was in danger. That he might lose more than just money.

That, in fact, Dr. Bashir might lose his life.

CHAPTER 4

Jake woke up with a gasp and a start. He sat up in bed, his heart pounding in alarm, but he saw nothing to be alarmed about. Morning light streamed in through the two windows. In the other bed, Nog, turned on his side with his back to Jake, slept on peacefully.

Yet something had wakened Jake, something that seemed wrong. Lying back against his pillow, Jake frowned and tried to put his finger on just what had happened—or not happened. Finally he smiled as he realized what had drawn him from sleep. He missed the constant low rumble he always heard aboard Deep Space Nine, the sound of all the station's systems working to keep the three hundred-odd people aboard safe and secure. At this early hour of the morning on Bajor, the only sounds were the gentle breeze and the occasional chirping of a native bird or insect.

Jake lay back and tried to go to sleep again, but the pull of adventure was too strong. At last he said, "Hey, Nog! Time to get up, don't you think?"

"Mmgh?" grumbled Nog.

Jake grinned. Nog was always boasting that Ferengi needed less sleep than Earth people, but apparently Ferengi were just as hard to wake up in the morning as Commander Sisko always swore Jake was. Jake grabbed his pillow and slammed it into Nog's head. "Get up!" he yelled, laughing.

Nog rolled out of bed, grabbed his own pillow, and threw it at Jake. Jake picked up the fallen weapon, jumped up onto the bed, and took a swing at Nog. Soon the boys had a full-scale pillow fight underway—more like a pillow war, really. Nog laughed and bellowed as he swung and was hit, and Jake was laughing out loud, too. Just as Jake drew back for a sweeping roundhouse pillow blow to Nog's head, though, the door opened suddenly.

"What is this?" demanded a quiet but firm voice.

Jake dropped the pillow, feeling guilty. A young Bajoran monk stood in the doorway, his face stern. "I must ask you to consider that other guests are sleeping," he said.

"Sorry," Jake mumbled.

Nog bowed deeply. "It is a ritual we go through upon awakening," he said smoothly. "It is our way of greeting a new day."

The young monk blinked uncertainly. "A ritual?" He scratched his head. "Oh, well, in that case, I—but it's so loud!"

Nog waved away the monk's objection. "We shall conduct the rite more quietly in the future," he said.

"Yes," Jake added. And he thought of something else to say: "We apologize for disturbing the serenity of the Tower of Hospitality."

"No apology is necessary," the monk said. "And

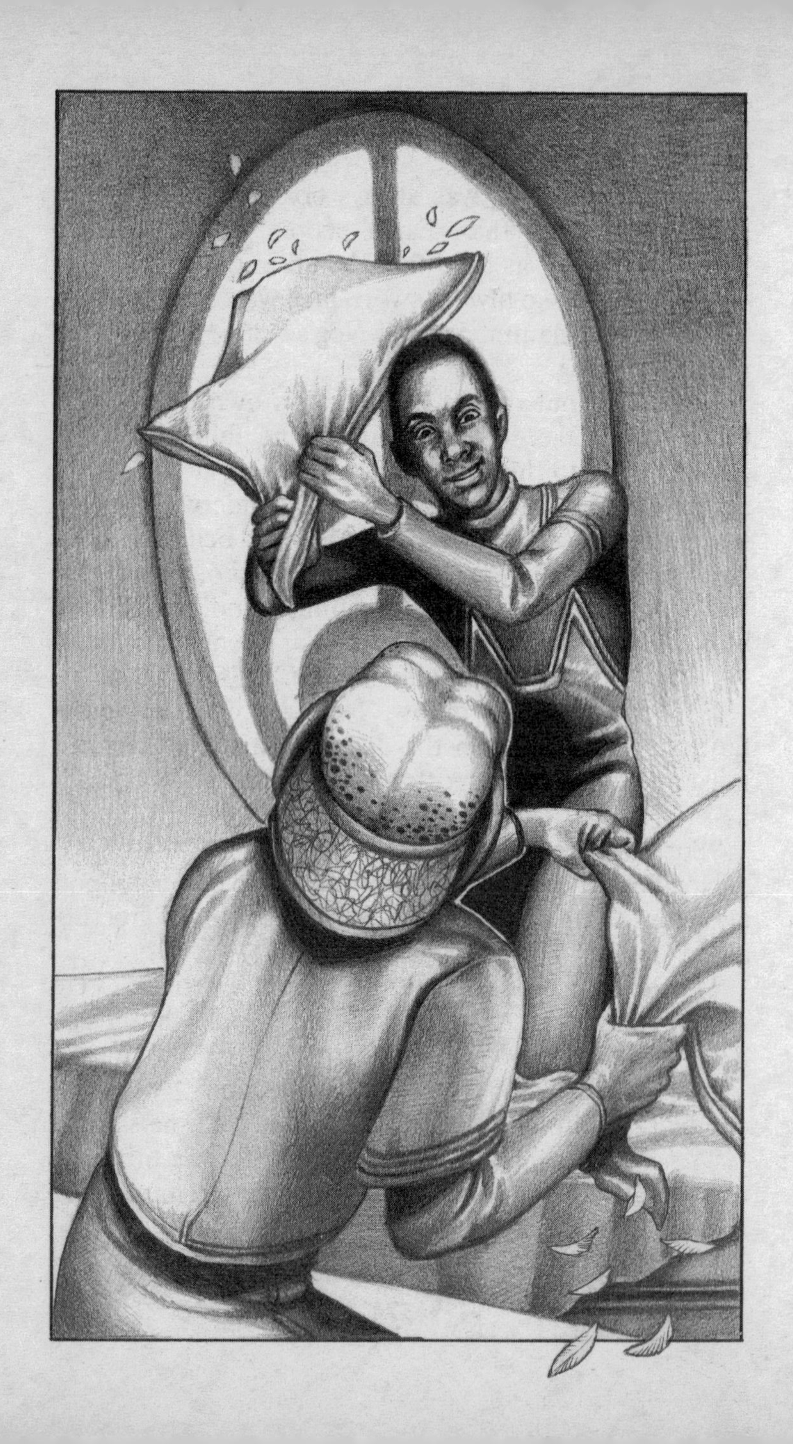

thank you for agreeing to conduct your ritual more quietly."

"Think nothing of it," Nog said grandly.

As soon as the monk closed the door, both boys burst into quiet laughter. "Quick thinking, Nog," Jake said, resisting the urge to roar out a belly laugh.

Nog waved his hand. "Monks are always easy to fool if you tell them whatever you're doing is a ritual," he said. "They have so many rites and rituals themselves, they're ready to believe everybody does. Well! I'm awake now. Shall we go out and eat, and then see what profit the day will bring?"

"Yes," Jake agreed. "I'm hungry."

They took turns under the shower. It was a weird experience for Jake, who had only rarely bathed in real water. The showers on Deep Space Nine, like those on the various Starfleet ships he had been on, were sonic, and they cleaned you without wetting you. But if the experience was weird, it was also new, and Jake was in the mood for new things.

On the way down they asked another monk if Dr. Bashir had come in. "No," the man told them. "I am certain he did not. Most strange—we expected him yesterday, and today there will surely be a demand for his room. It is festival time, you know."

Jake and Nog exchanged an uneasy glance, but neither of them said anything in front of the Bajoran. Jake was really worried now. They ate at a peddler's stall, munching some sort of toasty bread spread with sweet, soft fruit, and then they headed back to the plaza near the landing field. When Jake tried to talk about his concern,

Nog shrugged it off. "Nobody will hurt him," Nog said with confidence. "He's a Starfleet officer and a representative of the Federation. Everybody knows the Bajorans are eager to join the Federation."

"Not all of them," Jake insisted. He had often heard his father talk to his Bajoran aide, the pretty but intense Major Kira, about the political troubles of Bajor. The Cardassians had been cruel masters, and they had stolen most of Bajor's mineral wealth, but their presence on Bajor had had one good effect. It had unified all the Bajorans, if only in opposition to the Cardassians. Now that the hated Cardassians had abandoned the planet, old rivalries and hatreds had broken out again. The Bajoran Council, the nearest thing the planet had to a real planetary government, did desire membership in the Federation. Plenty of other Bajoran groups and individuals did not. Sometimes, Jake's father had said often, it seemed there were as many different Bajoran parties and factions as there were Bajorans.

All that morning Jake's uneasiness grew. While Nog was busy trading and bargaining, Jake slipped away to the landing area. The *Einstein* was still in its berth, along with a few other small ships. A Bajoran worker told Jake that he had not seen Dr. Bashir at all, which was odd because the doctor had said that he would return for his luggage. He never had.

Now badly worried, Jake went looking for Nog. He found the Ferengi hotly arguing with a Bajoran stallkeeper over the price of a few copper trinkets. As soon as Nog made his purchase, Jake dragged him away to a more or less quiet corner in the swirl of traffic. "I think Dr. Bashir's in trouble," Jake said.

With a wicked grin Nog said, "The Space Falcon? Never!"

"Come on," Jake said. "I'm not joking now. He hasn't been to the Hospitality Tower, and he hasn't even taken his luggage off the shuttle. That's not like him."

"He's having a great time somewhere," Nog insisted. "Now, I have my eye on some land-pearls in a shop down this street—"

Jake grabbed his arm. "Nog! You can't just go on as if nothing's happened. For all we know, that man Dr. Bashir went off with yesterday is some kind of criminal. We don't know anything about Tikar Antol—"

A girl's voice, sounding surprised and upset, cut in: "Tikar Antol? Did you say something about Tikar?"

Jake turned in surprise. Behind him stood the dark-haired Bajoran girl that Nog had noticed yesterday, the one with the jangling copper bracelets. She was carrying a basket of glowsilk scarves, and she was staring at the two boys. "Why?" Jake asked. "Do you know him? Do you know where we can find him?"

The girl took a step away from them. "Who are you? What have you to do with Tikar Antol?"

Nog put a hand on Jake's chest and pushed him aside. "Allow me," he said grandly. "Permit me to introduce ourselves. I am Nog the Magnificent, and this is my friend Jake the Grand. We are official representatives of the United Federation of Planets, and we—"

"Oh, stop it, Nog," Jake snapped. He turned to the girl. "We aren't really. I mean, we're from Deep Space Nine, but we're not official representatives of anything. I'm just plain Jake, and this is just Nog."

The girl was still looking at them suspiciously, but she

said, "My name is Sesana. I'm Atira Sesana. My father is Atira Meklat, a glowsilk merchant here in the bazaar." Bajoran family names, Jake remembered, came first, and personal names followed them.

Jake tried to guess her age. She was probably a year or so younger than he was, about thirteen in Earth years, but it was hard to tell with Bajorans. She could have been a little younger. "Listen, Sesana," Jake said, "we were talking about Tikar Antol because a friend of ours, also from Deep Space Nine, went off with him yesterday in a landtran, and we haven't seen either of them since."

"The Scar," Sesana said, her pale green eyes going wide with concern. "The Turnaway camp is somewhere in the Scar. That's where Tikar must have taken your friend."

"What is the Scar?" Nog asked.

"Walk with me. I have to take these scarves to a stall," Sesana said. The two boys walked on either side of her. Jake offered to carry her basket, but she thanked him and said it wasn't necessary. "It isn't heavy, and people in the bazaar might think you were trying to steal from me if they saw you take it. Everyone knows my father and me," she said.

"What is the Scar?" Nog asked again.

"It's a terrible wasteland," Sesana said. "Years ago the Cardassians carved a huge open pit into the ground there to mine for mineral ores."

"A strip mine," Jake said. He had read of such things in ecological histories. Back on Earth such mines had once threatened to ruin large stretches of territory. Fortunately, Earth mining operations gradually came to

be friendly to the environment, reseeding and replanting mined land. The Cardassians had never troubled themselves to do anything of the sort.

"It is a dead place," Sesana told them. "It goes on for a great distance, a desert of ravines and pools of poisonous water. Once it all was rich farmland, but now it is dead. It is the Scar."

They reached the merchant's stall where Sesana had to make her delivery. The Bajoran woman inside took the basket, pulled scarves from it, and held them up. The bright colors shimmered in the morning light. Then the woman stepped into a small enclosure and shut the door.

"What's she doing?" Nog asked.

"True glowsilk will give its own light in the dark," Sesana explained. "She is making sure that the scarves will really glow."

Nog looked greedy and interested. "Rare, are these scarves?"

"Oh, yes. They used to be very common, but the creatures that spin the silk were almost made extinct when the Cardassians ruined the islands where they lived. Now only a few farmers out on the islands raise them. None are left in the wild."

"Hmm," Nog said. "I would like to discuss these scarves with you—"

Just then the stallkeeper came out smiling. She signed a receipt that Sesana offered her, and then the girl led the boys away. Now that she was not carrying her basket, they moved more quickly through the crowd. "Why is Tikar Antol so dangerous?" Jake asked her.

She gave him a frightened glance. "I did not say that."

"No," Jake agreed, "but you look scared every time

someone mentions his name. Who is he, and why is he so horrifying?"

"Tikar Antol is a general," she said. "When the Cardassians ruled, he was one of the great leaders of the Resistance. But he is a bitter man. You may know that the Bajoran people are very religious. There are different sects, of course, but all of them are devoted to exploring the ways of the spirit. And all of them revered the Kai Opaka and her teachings—all but Tikar Antol and his Turnaways."

"And who are they?" Nog asked. "And about the glowsilk—"

"They say Tikar was the first Turnaway," Sesana replied. "He fought the Cardassians for years. They killed his whole family because of that—his father and mother, all his sisters and brothers, and his wife and children. The Cardassians tortured them horribly and then killed them. And Tikar lost his faith. He said if religion could not help him, if spiritual powers could not even protect his innocent wife and children, then he would turn away from them. And he did. His followers are also unbelievers."

"But the war with the Cardassians is over," objected Jake. "So why is Tikar still someone who scares you?"

"He frightens everyone!" Sesana exclaimed. "He does not want Bajor to join the Federation. None of his band do. And they all hate the Council because the Council follows the way of the Kai and the teachings of the priests. In other cities on Bajor there have been incidents—bombings, kidnappings, acts of terrorism. No one knows who is responsible, but all suspect the Turnaways. Around here Tikar is tolerated because he protected the people of the city during the Cardassian withdrawal, and because his army still exists. It is out there in the wilderness of the Scar, and no one knows how large it is. But everyone is afraid of the Turnaways and of their power, especially now."

"Now?" asked Jake.

"Because of that," Sesana said, nodding.

They had paused at an intersection. A crowd had gathered there, and they were murmuring in low voices. Passing by in the street was a procession of Bajoran monks in bright scarlet robes, ringing handbells and chanting a prayer. In the center of the throng walked a tall, balding man of fifty. His robe was silvery gray, and he lifted a hand in blessing as he passed by. Jake thought he looked like a kindly grandfather—a grandfather who carried a world of worry on his shoulders.

"Look out!" Nog suddenly shouted.

A young Bajoran had pushed through the crowd. He leapt out into the street, shoving his way through the startled band of monks. Jake gasped as he saw the young man raise a long, wickedly curved knife high, ready to strike at the old man—

And then the monks had closed in around him. They pushed him to the street as the crowd jostled this way and that, some trying to get out of the way, some trying to get a better view. One of the younger monks stood, his robe torn, his shoulder bloody. He held in his hand the curved knife. Others held the assassin down.

In a soft voice the old man in the silvery robe said, "Let him go. I forgive him."

"You are not a Vedek yet!" shouted the assassin.

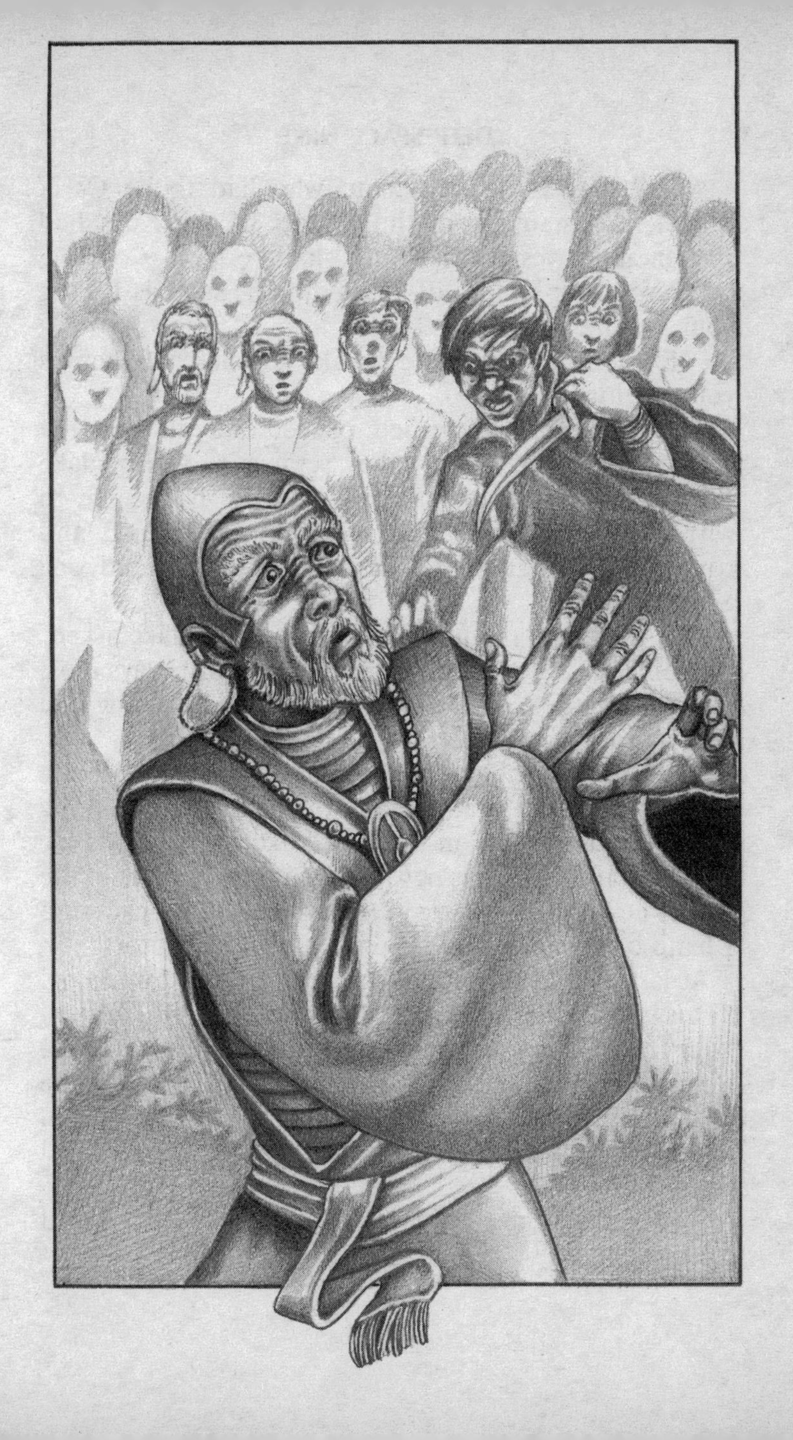

"No," agreed the old man, who had to be Carik Madal, the man whom the Keeper of the Keys had spoken about yesterday. "But I shall be."

"Despite the wishes of true Bajorans such as I!" the young man cried.

"Not despite you," said Carik. "Because of such as you. Let him go."

The young man, disarmed, pushed away through the crowd, going right past Jake, Sesana, and Nog. Jake shivered a little to think how close he had come to witnessing a murder. The procession re-formed and continued, with two monks helping the injured one along.

"Do they hate the new Vedek so much?" Jake asked.

"Some do," Sesana murmured. "The Turnaways most of all, because Carik Medal favors our joining the Federation."

They crossed the street and made their way through the crowds of Bajorans, many of them loudly talking about the assassination attempt. Jake found that they did not travel as fast as news—or rumors, for lots of the stories he overheard had multiplied the one attacker into a band of men armed with phasers and disruptors.

At last Sesana stopped in front of a domed building. "This is my father's place of business," she said. "Listen: Your friend is in great danger if he has gone with Tikar. He may be a prisoner of the Turnaways. They despise the Federation, and they will do anything to keep Bajor from joining it. You must go to the authorities at once. Tell them that—"

"We can't," Jake said. "Uh, we're kind of illegal ourselves."

She blinked at them. "You are from Deep Space Nine," she said. "The local constables have no power over you."

"Jake," Nog said in a warning voice. "Maybe we'd better just—"

"We stowed away," Jake said. "We'll be in trouble—and I'm not sure that anything happened to the doctor, anyway. He went along with Tikar willingly, and he looked fine then. Maybe you could help us check this out."

"You don't know what you are asking," Sesana said. "The Turnaways wouldn't hesitate to kill us all—"

"Oh, well, we can go back to the shuttle and call for help," Nog said. "Sorry to have bothered you. Bye now."

"Nog," Jake said, stepping in front of his friend to keep him from strolling away. "We can't call Deep Space Nine. What if Dr. Bashir is all right? Anything might have happened. He might even have come across some medical emergency that's keeping him away. If nothing is wrong with him, we'll look like fools. Anyway, remember that Dad isn't on the station right now. Do you want Major Kira to punish us?"

Nog swallowed hard. Major Kira, too, had been a Bajoran freedom fighter. She had very little use for pranks. "All right," he said reluctantly. "We'll see what we can do. But we will need some help."

"Sesana?" asked Jake. "I know we have no business asking you, but could you tell us the way?"

She shook her head. "You'll never get there," she said. She gave her father's business place a longing look. Then she took a deep breath. "Oh, very well. My mother and father fought against the Cardassians. I suppose their daughter can fight against the Turnaways. Come with me. I have a way to get us to the Scar."

"Thank you," Jake said.

She glared at him, anger flashing in her green eyes. "Just wait!" she snapped. "After we come back, then you can thank me. If we come back alive, that is."

CHAPTER 5

Sesana led them through a maze of twisting, narrow streets between shabby buildings. Nog seemed torn between his attraction to Sesana and his wish to make money. He kept looking back the way they had come with longing. "Maybe you two should try to find the doctor while I stay back in the bazaar," he said once. "If he should show up, I can spot him and—"

"He won't be back," Sesana said firmly. "Not if he is in the Turnaways' hands."

They came to a large unpaved square where wagons rumbled past, drawn by the green horned animals. A fine pall of yellow dust hung in the air. "What are those creatures?" Nog asked, stepping aside as two of the animals padded toward him, a heavy wagon trundling along behind.

Sesana glanced at them. "Those are fabors," she said. "Draft animals from the desert. They need little water. We won't be taking them, though."

"We're taking an animal?" Nog asked, looking

alarmed. He was small, much shorter than Jake, and he did not like large creatures anywhere around him.

"We're taking my lopp," she said. "The stable is over here."

Jake blinked as they stepped from the bright sunlight into the dim interior of a domed stable. Dry grass littered the floor and crunched underfoot, giving off a sweet scent. In the darkness, some large animals breathed noisily, and occasionally one would make a long, rattling, gargling noise. "He's back here," said Sesana, leading them to the darkest part of the building.

Now that his eyes were getting accustomed to the dimness, Jake could see stalls on either side. Graceful necks craned out of some of them. They reminded Jake of Earth horses—if horses had leathery brown skin and a sawtoothed row of spines growing on their necks instead of manes. Deep-set, dark eyes gleamed at them as they passed. Sesana stopped finally at one of the stalls and swung the wood-and-rope gate open. "Come on, Whitefoot," she crooned softly. With a snort the large animal came out.

Nog gulped and stepped back, and Jake moved away a little, too. Whitefoot was muscular and imposing, its shoulder almost level with the top of Jake's head. The big brown animal had large, flat white feet at the end of four strong, knobby-kneed legs. Whitefoot smoothly lowered its head, and Sesana slipped some kind of bridle over it. "We won't saddle him," she said. "I don't have a three-person saddle, so we'll make do with a simple riding pad. But we'll put a water sling on him. Jake, you take these containers out to the fountain and fill them."

She handed Jake a net with four empty leather bottles

attached to its corners. Jake slung it over his shoulder and went outside. At the center of the unpaved plaza was a tall stone fountain, with several sets of steps approaching it. He climbed one set and saw that others were filling similar water bottles. A Bajoran moved aside for him, and Jake imitated the way the Bajoran held the leather bottles under the trickling water. The flow was cold over his hands.

The Bajoran smiled at him. "Short trip," he said.

"Uh—yeah," Jake said.

"Well, don't get lost. Four water bottles won't last long out there," the Bajoran said with a nod toward an arched gate.

"I'll be careful," Jake said.

He lugged the four full bottles back to the stables. Sesana was waiting there impatiently, and Nog had retreated to a safe distance from the lopp. Sesana had tossed a plush riding pad over the creature's back. Now she was stroking the earless head and murmuring softly to Whitefoot. When Jake handed over the net with the water bottles, she climbed up on a fence next to the lopp and swung the net over the animal's back. The lopp grunted and shook its head. "Come on," Sesana said as she threw her leg over the animal's back. "You can sit behind me, and then Nog."

"Me?" squeaked Nog. "Uh—look, I think I'd really rather stay here and—"

"Come on, Nog," Jake said firmly.

The Ferengi swallowed hard. "I'm going to regret this," he muttered, but he came slowly forward.

Jake climbed the fence and clambered onto Whitefoot's back. The animal shifted restlessly, and Jake had to grab hold of Sesana's waist to keep from tumbling off.

"No," she said. "Hang on to the net. That's safer. If you fall off, at least I will stay on."

Great, thought Jake. He was sitting on the net, which Sesana had attached to the riding pad. He seized the mesh and looked back at Nog, who was hesitating at the fence. Jake said, "Come on. It's easy." He held out his hand. "Here, grab hold and I'll help you. No, give me your other hand."

At last Nog scrambled aboard, and Sesana clucked to Whitefoot. The animal lurched forward. "Whoa!" Nog shouted, swaying wildly from side to side. "I'll fall!"

"Hold on," Sesana said impatiently. "You'll get used to it."

Whitefoot lumbered out beneath the arched gate, and they were on a rough, graveled road. Ahead of them in the distance wagons swayed and clattered and raised clouds of yellow dust. Close to Sakelo City the landscape was green. Spiky grasslike plants and glossy deep green vines covered rolling hills. In the distance, though, the sun glared on bare yellow hillsides. They headed that way, swerving out onto a bare track away from the main road. "The Scar," Sesana said, her voice grim. "Nothing lives there now. They say the Turnaways have a camp there, somewhere, with food domes and deep wells. At least they used to have a camp there, back when they were fighting the Cardassians."

As Whitefoot lumbered along, Jake and even Nog gradually got used to the swaying gait. At least they wouldn't fall off—though Jake knew his rear end would be sore for days after the uncomfortable ride. An hour out from Sakelo City they came to a hillside that sloped down away from them. "This is where the Cardassian mining operation began," Sesana said. "You see what they did."

Jake took a deep breath. They were on the rim of a vast crater, a crater so wide that the other side was out of sight. Nothing grew there that he could see—it was just a jumbled, barren wasteland, cut by deep ravines and dotted with gray boulders. Here and there poisonous-looking green pools of water shimmered under the brassy sky. "They're out there?" Nog asked, awe in his voice. "How will we ever find them?"

"They'll find us, more likely," Sesana muttered. "But I've heard my father talk about the old days. He says the rebels used to come out from Fanto's Rip to attack the Cardassians. That's where we're going." She urged Whitefoot forward.

Jake clutched fistfuls of the animal's hair desperately as they went downhill. The slope was much deeper than he had thought at first. By the time the lopp had leveled out again, they were a good thousand feet lower than they had been. Like a huge, shallow bowl, the Scar sloped away from them, dropping away to an unknown level somewhere out under the baking sun.

"One good thing," Sesana said. "If Tikar Antol came here in a landtran, then I know the way he must have taken into Fanto's Rip. There aren't many roads down into the Scar, and there's only one that leads close to the Rip. So we'll come in from that direction."

"We saw them leave in a landtran, anyway," Jake

muttered. Sweat stung his eyes. It was getting hotter and hotter. Sakelo City was in the tropics of Bajor, and the sun was intense. "What exactly is the Rip?"

The Rip, Sesana explained, was a ravine cut by erosion. It led to the Deadly Lake, a wide, shallow expanse of poisonous water at the center of the Scar. "The Cardassians had finished with this section of the Scar when the erosion started," Sesana said. "They didn't care. The story is that one of the sub-prefects, Gul Fanto, used to dump the bodies of slaves who had died from overwork into the ravine. So it came to be called after him. Now it's a deep gorge, and they say that the rebel camp is somewhere inside it, but cloaked."

"Cloaked?" said Nog. "What do you mean, cloaked?"

"A Bajoran rebel stole a small Cardassian spaceship, and then captured a Romulan vessel," Sesana told him. "It was a famous exploit. The Romulan ship was badly damaged, but the rebel flew it back to the planet here and brought down the cloaking device. Tikar Antol wound up in possession of it. Thanks to the cloaking device, the Cardassians were never able to find the Turnaway camp."

Nog grunted. "Oh, great. And now we're out looking for it. By the profits of my ancestors, I wish I'd never left Deep Space Nine."

They stopped twice for sips of water, and then they continued west in a curving track that led them deeper and deeper into the Scar. From time to time they passed silent evidence of the Cardassian occupation: temporary storage buildings, rusted to ruin, molybidenal landing pads blown over with drifts of fine yellow sand, mineshafts choked with rubble. At last, three hours after they had entered the Scar, Sesana reined in Whitefoot. "We're close to the Rip," she said. "I think we had better approach on foot."

"Finally!" Nog said.

"I think we had better speak very quietly, too," Sesana warned.

They slipped off Whitefoot's back. Jake's thighs ached, and his legs felt weak. Nog could hardly stand at first. After some stamping and groaning, though, he said he was ready to go. They drank some water—it had become warm and unappetizing in the heat of the sun—and then they went carefully forward. They came up over a low rise, and Sesana pointed. "There is the road," she said in a whisper.

Jake shaded his eyes and squinted. The "road" was more like a bare scrape, unpaved and narrow, winding between boulders and low bare hills. They approached it, and then Sesana handed Whitefoot's bridle to Jake. "Hold him," she said. "I want to take a look." She walked over to the roadside and then slowly followed the road for several hundred yards, with Jake and Nog trailing along behind. Whitefoot didn't think much of Jake as a rein-holder. The big animal kept jerking his head and breathing hot, moist air on Jake's neck and cheek. Finally Sesana pointed. "Yes," she said. "The wind took most of the track, but see here."

Jake craned his neck to look. In the protected area behind a boulder a small patch of sand held the criss-cross pattern of a landtran tread. "That must be the track that Tikar left," he said.

"Yes," agreed Sesana. "It's at least a day old. But even better, there aren't any outgoing tracks. That means that Tikar is still there—and your friend must be there, too."

They walked parallel to the road for what seemed to Jake like a very long time. At last they saw ahead the lip of a cliff that dropped away from them as far as they could see in either direction. "That is the Rip," Sesana said, though Jake had already guessed that much.

He was impressed. He knew that this part of Bajor had two seasons, a dry season and a rainy one. They were halfway through the dry season now, and it was hard to believe that for half the Bajoran year the Sakelo City area was drenched by pouring, lashing storms. Now, however, Jake could easily believe it. Only huge floods could have gouged out this tremendous gorge, cutting through sand and stone.

The Rip was at least a kilometer across, more than half a mile. As they neared the rim, Jake could see that it dropped down for more than two hundred meters, nearly a thousand feet. The walls were streaked with red, orange, white, and gray layers of stone, and jumbles of stone at the bottom of the V-shaped gorge showed where there had been landslides. It looked desolate and fearsome.

The sun was sliding down the sky, and afternoon shadows were stretching long when Sesana pointed ahead. "There," she said. "There's something."

Jake looked forward. "I don't see anything."

Sesana pointed again. "There, just past those rocks. Aren't those footprints?"

Now that he knew where to look, Jake could discern

faint disturbances in the sand, marks that made a track leading over the edge of the gorge. "Nog," Jake whispered, "can you hear anything?"

Poor Nog looked all in. He was panting with the heat, and he groaned miserably. But he stood listening intently, moving his head from side to side. "I don't even hear a bug," he said at last. "Just the wind down in the gorge."

They crept forward, cautiously. Although from a distance it had looked as if the footprints went right over the edge of a sheer drop, they now saw that there was a rough track down the side of the ravine here, a sort of ledge that led steeply down the face of the cliff. It might be artificial, made by the Bajoran rebels, or it might be a natural ledge—it was impossible to tell.

"We're lucky," whispered Sesana.

"Lucky?" croaked Nog in a disbelieving voice.

"If the Turnaways had been as careful as they used to be, they would have swept out their footprints," Sesana explained. "Then we would never have found this way down. The road leads down into the Rip farther along, but I'm sure it will be well guarded. This may be a back way in." She looked at the two friends. "All right," she said. "This is your last chance. Do we go back to Sakelo and call in the constables?"

Before Nog could speak, Jake said, "No. It's up to us."

"All right," Sesana said. "Here we go. It will have to be single file."

"Nog had better go first," Jake said. "He can hear anyone ahead of us before you or I could see them."

"Thank you, my friend," Nog grumbled. "Anything to

get out of this heat!" He went forward and moaned as he looked down the ledge. "I don't like heights," he complained.

"Don't look into the ravine," advised Sesana. "Just keep your eyes on the track."

Nog looked most unhappy, but he cautiously descended. Sesana followed, leading Whitefoot. Jake blinked at how rapidly they vanished from sight. The track was very steep. He took a last glance around the desolate landscape of the Scar, swallowed hard, wished his heart was not thudding so loudly, and followed his friends down into the unknown dangers of the Rip.

CHAPTER 6

The narrow, rocky track led down at a steep angle. Sometimes it had almost worn away, and the three of them had to hug the cliff face to inch along. Sometimes a stone gave way under Jake's foot and went bumping and thudding and crashing down, the small sound loud and echoing in the desert silence of the Rip. Soon Jake felt exhausted, sweating and gasping the hot air and trying to blink away the grit and dirt that the light breeze kept blowing in his face.

"Here," Sesana said once when they had paused on a wider ledge. She handed him a colorful scarf.

When Jake wiped his face with it, he felt the grime that had stuck to him. He sighed and looked at Nog, who had all but wilted under the heat. Nog's bald head had a fine layer of dust on it, too, and he was panting for breath. "How much farther is it?" Nog asked with a groan.

Sesana shook her head. "I do not know. I have no map, and there are only legends to tell of the Turnaways and their camp."

"Great," Nog muttered. "We'll come walking right into their open arms."

"I don't think so," Sesana told him. "You see, no one uses this track anymore. The Turnaways carved it out so their animals and vehicles could pass into and out of the Rip, but the Cardassians discovered it, so the rebels abandoned it. You can see how it has washed and fallen away. Once or twice I have been down here, looking for anthrolite crystals."

Nog looked more lively. "Anthrolite crystals? What are they?"

With a smile Sesana said, "Nothing special. They are like little pyramids of orange fire. Sometimes they occur in ore deposits, but they have no practical value, so the Cardassians never took them. I like to make jewelry from them, though. Here, I have one—see?" She drew a necklace from inside her tunic. Jake saw dangling from it a little glittering orange-red crystal, flashing brightly in the sun.

Nog's gaze grew greedy. "Ah," he said. "Maybe I could sell a few of these on Deep Space Nine—"

Jake sighed and said, "Nog, we're trying to find Dr. Bashir, remember?"

Sounding irritated, Nog said, "I know, I know. But what's wrong with combining a little pleasure with rescue? Now, if we could find some of these anthrolites—"

Sesana had filled a soft canteen with water. Jake drank from it and tossed it to Nog. "Here. Have a drink, and then we have to go on with the search. You can worry about your sales later."

Nog grumbled and complained, but he took a long swallow of water and got to his feet again. The three resumed their downward march. As they descended, the cliff cut off the direct rays of the sun, and the heat grew a little more bearable. Still, the path was uncertain and treacherous. Sesana warned the boys against making too much noise, and Jake had to watch where he put his feet—it wouldn't do for him to send a rock crashing down into the ravine, because they were getting very near the bottom of the trail and someone down there might hear it.

The rocky floor of the Rip was a wasteland of bare stone and blowing sand. A hot breeze gusted through it, whipping up little dancing whirlwinds. Here and there the stone had been melted, and it had flowed into odd-looking orange-yellow puddles, where it had cooled and hardened again. Jake thought it looked like some kind of pudding that had been plopped down and frozen in place. Hardly any life showed up here. Jake saw occasional spiky green desert plants, like clusters of bayonets. A tough, wiry kind of yellow-green moss grew on the shady side of some of the boulders. Every now and then a scurrying black Bajoran insect, the size of an Earth ant but equipped with ten legs, would dart across their path. Aside from these, Jake could see no indication that anyone had been here since the Cardassians had left Bajor.

"Is that melted rock from mining?" Jake asked Sesana in a whisper.

"No. Battle," she replied.

Jake gulped and looked around. The puddles of melted and rehardened stone lay everywhere. From the size of them, the Cardassians must have been using starship-class phaser fire. He tried to imagine what it must have been like for the rebels, hiding here with great explosions of white-hot liquid rock bursting up around them. In his imagination he saw the small band of Bajoran freedom fighters, armed with personal weapons, hiding behind boulders. And from up above, perhaps from the rim of the ravine, came the searing phaser blasts that could vaporize flesh and bone. It must have been a terrible, one-sided fight. No wonder the Bajorans made heroes of the rebels, even of the unbelievers, the Turnaways.

Finally the trail leveled out. They were on the floor of the ravine now, and looking back, Jake had a moment of dizziness. They had come down a trail at least three kilometers long. From here it looked like the smallest possible scratch on the ravine wall. And the climb out, Jake thought grimly, would be even more difficult than the descent.

The ravine twisted and turned and fell away before them. They descended an uneven slope and came suddenly on water and life. A round green pool, maybe twenty meters across—about sixty-five feet or so—lay with its surface rippled by the gusting breezes. Tough, spiky grasses grew along its edge, and Jake glimpsed something, some fishlike life-form, darting beneath the surface.

"It is pretty," Sesana said, "but the water is poisonous to people. This is a rain pond—the yearly rains fill it to five or six times its depth now, and then it shrinks to less than half this size in the dry season. The poisons collect as the water runs through the ravine. The only safe water down here comes from the deep springs—and no one but the Turnaways knows where those springs are."

"Note," Nog muttered. "Do not drink the water."

They passed the pool and headed even farther down the ravine. After an hour or so had passed, Nog, who was still leading the way, suddenly stopped in his tracks, his pose intent. "I hear something," he whispered.

Jake listened, but for the life of him he could hear nothing except the faint rush of the wind through the ravine. But then, he reflected, he did not have Nog's listening equipment. "What is it?" he asked Nog in a low voice.

Not tilted his head a little. "Someone is coming down into the canyon," he murmured. "I hear the clatter and scrape of boots. Sounds like ten or twelve people, at least. And I think their path is even steeper than ours was."

"We will have to be careful—and silent," Sesana warned.

They crept along. Then, as they came around an outcrop of rock, Jake saw them. Several figures, at least a dozen and possibly more, were climbing down the face of the cliff, along a scratch that was even narrower and steeper than the one they had used. He squinted. Although they were far away, he could tell that the people climbing down held on to a rope or cable of some kind. Nog closed his eyes in concentration.

The climbers reached the floor of the ravine and walked away, vanishing around a curve. "Well?" Jake asked Nog.

"Recruits, most of them," Nog said. "It seems that the new Vedek is not popular with these people. They were complaining that a friend of theirs tried to kill him and failed. That must have been what we saw. But three of these people were talking like leaders. I get the idea that the new ones are going to be taken to the camp for training. That was about all I could make out."

"We'd better not get too far behind," Sesana said.

The three made their way forward, tense and ready to jump at a shadow. At last they came to a place where rockslides had almost blocked the floor of the ravine. Only a narrow channel was open. "I don't like the look of that," Jake said. "It could be a trap."

"Yes—or a sentry post," Sesana replied. They moved to one side and found a place where they could scramble up the slope of jumbled boulders left by a slide.

As Jake raised his eyes over the summit, he blinked in surprise. There, a kilometer or more away from them, was a city, a secret city hidden within the Rip. He could see tents and structures made of what looked like scrap metal. Landtrans stood here and there, and people milled about in the "streets" between the tents and the buildings. On the slopes at either side of the ravine stood rusty-looking round metal tanks and a few metal buildings that might once have been warehouses or storage bins. Passing right through the center of all this, at the lowest point of the ravine floor, was a deep channel, bridged here and there by narrow planks or by arches of stone. And something was wrong with the sky above the hidden city.

The sky wavered and shimmered. It was like looking through waves of heat, but heat did not cause the shimmering. Jake knew he must be seeing the effects of a cloaking device, but from the inside. If the cloaking device worked the way they did in space, then no observer from above could see the camp at all—or even detect it with sensors. If the Cardassians had tried to find the camp from space or even from low-level flights, they would have failed.

And yet Jake realized that hundreds of people lived there, perhaps even a thousand or more. It was a formidable fighting force, especially when you considered the hit-and-run style favored by the Bajoran freedom fighters. Jake had heard Major Kira tell stories about her own days as an underground fighter on Bajor. Although she had lived on another continent, far away from the Scar and the Rip, she had stories of stealthy raids, sabotage, and even assassination that made Jake appreciate how deadly the Turnaway camp could have been during the Bajoran occupation.

And how deadly it could be even now.

The three friends looked at the camp and then ducked back down behind the protecting boulders. "Do you think your doctor is in there?" asked Sesana. She looked strained and frightened.

"I don't know," Jake admitted. "But if that's where Tikar Antol went, then the chances are that Dr. Bashir is there, too."

"What do we do now?" Nog asked. "There are only three of us. We can't just go charging into there. They'd grab us at once."

Sesana bit her lip. "There's only one way," she said. "Maybe I can slip into the camp."

"No!" Jake said, almost forgetting to whisper. "You're crazy. You couldn't possibly get away with it."

"Why not?"

Jake shifted his weight uncomfortably. He felt like a lizard on the face of the jumbled boulders. "Well, you're too young," he muttered. "And you don't have any training for this kind of thing. And you're a—well, you're just a girl."

Sesana glared at him. "My mother was no older than I when she slit the throat of a Cardassian executioner," she said. "And she was just a girl, too, or so they thought."

"Still," Jake said. "There must be another way."

Sesana shook her head. "No. Don't you see, Jake? I am the only one of us who could possibly get inside the camp and hope to be unnoticed. I may be a girl, and I may be young, but I am also something else."

"What is that?" Nog asked.

"I am a Bajoran," Sesana said simply. "And you, Nog, have told us that the Turnaways are taking in Bajoran recruits. I do not think they have any Ferengi or humans among their number. So it has to be me."

"I don't like it," Jake said.

Sesana smiled bitterly. "Do you think I like it? Still, it is our only chance. If only we can spot a time when I can make it in."

They hid themselves there for a long time. Bajor's seasons, like those of Earth, affected the length of the day. It was summer now in this part of Bajor, and the days were very long. But late that afternoon, the chance finally came. Nog heard the approach of another group, and as he listened, he told the others that these, too, were new recruits.

They hid close to the path. Soon the newcomers came into sight. It was a group of sixteen Bajorans—only one

Turnaway leader, Nog had told them, which was fortunate for them, and fifteen brand-new recruits, both men and women. All were dressed in the ordinary Bajoran style, so Sesana wouldn't stand out among them. The group came past their hiding place, and Sesana slipped away. She fell into step at the rear, and none of the Bajorans, still hot and exhausted from their climb down the ravine, noticed her. By the time the recruits passed through the narrow opening between the rockslides, Jake could no longer tell Sesana apart from the others. He hoped her cover would hold.

"Now what?" Nog asked.

"You heard the plan," Jake said. They had worked it out during the long hours of waiting. Sesana would go into the camp, find out what she could about any prisoners—particularly any human prisoners—and would try to make her way back out after nightfall. The boys were to wait for her here, and if she did not return by dawn, they were to go back to town and spread the alarm.

Nog shook his head. "I think we have made a mistake," he told Jake.

"Yeah," agreed Jake. "I feel bad about letting her go in there all alone."

"I know what you mean," Nog said. "I should have offered to hold her anthrolite necklace for her."

Jake scowled at Nog.

Nog shifted uncomfortably under Jake's frown. "Well," he said defensively, "I only mean that if she doesn't come back again, that would be *something* that would bring a little profit."

With a sigh Jake said, "Nog, we are going to take shifts

keeping watch. I will take the first one. You rest until I ask you to replace me. And then you will watch. And until Sesana gets safely back, I don't want to hear another word about profits. If I do, then I'll do something nasty to you."

"You wouldn't hit me," Nog said. "I'm your friend."

"I wouldn't hit you," Jake agreed. "No, I'd just tell your father that you gave me a present. For free."

Nog gasped. "You wouldn't!"

"Don't try me," Jake said. "Settle down now. I've got the first watch."

Nog tried to make himself as comfortable as possible, sitting with his back against a boulder. Jake climbed a little higher, concealing himself between two huge rocks. He could just see the camp from here. The recruits had passed under the cloaking effect. They were just a small group of figures now, impossible to tell apart from the many others. But somewhere in there was Sesana, and Jake hoped that she would come back again safe and sound. If not—

Well, if not, Jake had no idea what to do next.

CHAPTER 7

That afternoon Jake saw lots of activity from his vantage point. A squad of Bajorans came out of the cloaked compound and onto a round, sandy level spot on the far side of the Rip. Jake thought that once, before the rockslides had choked the canyon, the sandy spot probably had been a seasonal pool, like the ones they had seen earlier.

Jake had been studying the landscape, and he had concluded that the Turnaways had done some clever engineering. During the rainy season, torrents of water would come pouring down the Rip. The rockslides would hold some of it back. They made a partial dam that would look natural from the air, as if part of the ravine walls had simply collapsed. But the Turnaways must have triggered the slides, because they served another purpose.

They would direct the floods of water to the deep channel cut through the Turnaway camp. Jake could imagine the canyon in flood season, with foaming brown water pouring through the narrow opening between the rockslides. From there the water would gush into the artificial channel, and then the center of the camp would have a sort of canal through it. At the lower end presumably the canal opened out again into the ravine. All this would help the Turnaways. After all, an enemy might reason, it would be impossible to establish a permanent camp in the path of an annual flood.

Now Jake wished he had a pair of binoculars. He could see the distant Bajorans on the sandy, round field going through some kind of exercises. He guessed they were learning personal combat skills, but he was too far away to see any details. A smaller group some distance from the first was obviously undergoing target practice. Jake saw the beams of phaser fire and the puffs of vapor where they struck the cliff side, where targets must have been set up. It was just too far for him to see anything clearly, though.

Suddenly someone laid a hand on Jake's shoulder. He jerked with alarm—and then he saw it was only Nog. "You scared me half to death!" Jake whispered. "What's wrong?"

"Nothing," Nog said, grinning with his sharp teeth. "I got bored, that's all. What's going on?"

Jake nodded across the ravine. "Practice, looks like. Can you hear anything?"

Nog listened for a few moments. "Too far even for me," he said. "All I can hear are some shouts of encouragement from the wrestlers, and the sizzling sound of the phasers when they hit the rock."

"I guess you can't tell if Sesana is in either group," Jake said, feeling disappointed.

"Sorry," Nog replied. He slipped down the slope and

stretched his arms and legs. "You know, what I can't figure out is why the Turnaways would want Dr. Bashir in the first place."

"Huh?" Jake asked.

"Think about it," Nog insisted. "They don't want what's-his-name, Carik, to be a Vedek. All right, that's their privilege. I mean, the Federation never interferes in the politics of a planet anyway, as long as they're local and don't threaten other planets. So even if old Tikar wants to kill Carik before this Vedek ceremony, that's a local concern. What are they going to do with Dr. Bashir—have him take on Carik as a patient and treat him to death?"

Jake turned that over in his mind. He had been so worried about Dr. Bashir's safety that he had not even asked himself the questions that Nog was raising, but his friend had a point. Although Bashir had concealed his true identity from Tikar, the Turnaway leader had to know that his captive was human. In this sector, that meant he must come from Deep Space Nine. Surely Tikar Antol must know that he had no need for a Starfleet hostage. Even if Tikar succeeded in assassinating a local religious leader, Starfleet could do nothing—not unless the Bajoran Council formally requested aid. And that was something the disorganized, squabbling council would not do. It made very little sense.

Jake said slowly, "Maybe they want Dr. Bashir for something else. Maybe it doesn't have anything to do with the Vedek at all."

"Maybe," suggested Nog with a yawn. "Maybe Tikar's going into the spy business, and he needs the Space Falcon to show him the ropes."

Jake shook his head. "That doesn't seem funny anymore, Nog."

"Humor," said Nog, "is a matter of opinion."

They had nothing to do but wait, and waiting was hard. Nog took over from Jake at twilight, and Jake tried to rest. He had no chance of going to sleep, of course, but his legs ached from the long trek down into the ravine, and he wanted the chance just to close his eyes for a few minutes. He quickly discovered that getting comfortable was impossible. The boulders were jagged and rough, and no matter how he leaned, a sharp little piece was sure to stick him in the back. He could not lie down on the sand, because there simply wasn't enough sand here in their hiding place. He didn't dare move away from the spot, either, because Sesana was returning here. Besides, in the gathering dusk he was uncomfortably certain that he would get lost in no time.

So he just sat there, shifting his weight and feeling miserable. Overhead the sky grew dark, and a few stars appeared. Looking up at them, Jake reflected that living out there, in space, was not so bad after all. Maybe Deep Space Nine could be dull at times, but his room was always comfortable, at least. And there his father, the big, reliable Commander Sisko, was in charge, and Jake didn't have all the worry and concern of trying to keep track of the wayward Dr. Bashir. It was strange, though, sitting here on a planet and wishing he were back on the station. Only a day earlier he had been on the station wishing he were on the planet. Jake sighed. Life just wasn't fair, and that was all there was to it.

"Sst!" hissed Nog from up above. "Someone's coming!"

Jake sprang up and tensed his muscles. "Where?" he whispered.

"Coming through the path between the rockslides," Nog replied. "Running." After a moment Nog spoke again, sounding relieved. "It's okay. It's just Sesana."

Jake had been holding his breath. He let it out in a long sigh of relief. He expected her right away, but it was five more minutes before she came close enough for him to hear, and another minute before he saw her, a dark shape moving through the night. She came straight to them. "We have to move," she said. "They have a tracking field inside the compound, and I may have tripped it when I left. Follow me!"

Running after her was a nightmare for Jake. He stumbled, tripped, and stubbed his toes about a dozen times. They retreated to a place a kilometer or so up the canyon. Then Sesana asked Nog to listen for pursuit. "Nothing," the Ferengi boy reported after a few seconds. "I hope you brought us some food. I'm starving!"

To Jake's surprise, Sesana had brought them food, some hard-packed fruit bread. The taste was sweet and tangy, and a little of it filled Jake up. They swallowed water to wash it down. "Good," Nog said. "What was that?"

"It's ration bread," Sesana told him. "Lots of calories, lots of energy. I have enough for one more meal for us all. But listen! I found out about Dr. Bashir."

"You did?" Jake asked. He had been feeling tired before Sesana showed up, but now he was ready for action. "What about him?"

"He's in the camp, all right," Sesana said. "There's a stone hut back from the other buildings, up near the fuel tanks. That's where they're keeping him." She lowered her voice and went on: "Everything is all confused in the camp. It turns out that Tikar Antol is in trouble. He has lost lots of his followers, and lots of the others want to leave the band now that the Cardassians have gone away. He's using this business of the new Vedek to draw more people in. That is lucky for us. I'd guess more than half the camp is made up of new recruits who don't know the rules yet, so it was easy for me to slip around."

"Yes, but what about Dr. Bashir?" demanded Jake impatiently.

"I'm coming to that," Sesana returned. "You have to understand a few things to begin with. First, Tikar plans to assassinate Carik Madal—but *after* Carik is named Vedek, not before. He was terribly angry when he found out a young hothead had already made an attempt on Carik's life. I think he's ordered that the young man be killed."

"What?" Nog asked. "When they both want the same thing?"

Jake said nothing. He remembered the grandfatherly Carik Madal leaning over the young man and saying, "I forgive you." He reflected that Bajorans were complicated people. On one side, you had the old man who could forgive his attacker. On the other, you had Tikar Antol, who could kill a man just as an example to others.

Sesana was talking: "They don't really want the same thing," she was saying to Nog. "The assassin was just someone who was disappointed in the choice of Carik Madal. He wanted his own candidate to be named Vedek and to sit on the Council. But Tikar wants Carik dead just as a stepping stone to more power. He wants to control the Council himself. Tikar wants to run all of Bajor."

"What about Dr. Bashir?" Jake urged again.

"I'm coming to that," insisted Sesana. "I heard some guards talking about him. I gather from what they said that someone at the landing field is a Turnaway spy. He reported that Dr. Bashir was on his way the moment he left the space station. The Turnaways knew from the beginning who Dr. Bashir was and that he came from Deep Space Nine. That is why they need him, but the doctor is not cooperating. Tikar is very angry. He tried to bully Dr. Bashir into taking a delegation of Turnaways up to Deep Space Nine, but Dr. Bashir refused. So now Tikar has sent for his own doctor, a Bajoran Turnaway who specialized in torture back during the Cardassian occupation."

"T-torture?" croaked Nog.

Jake felt cold. "What are they going to do to him?" he asked.

After a moment of silence Sesana said, "I'm not sure. I think they are going to drug him and then let him fly his shuttle back to Deep Space Nine. Do either of you know what a vandellium device is?"

"No," Nog said.

But Jake knew. Suddenly he felt not only cold, but chilled to the bone. "It's an outlawed device of war," he said, his voice shaking. "It isn't an ordinary bomb. It explodes without any real destructive force. You could probably sit in a chair beside one when it went off, and the explosion would barely be great enough to knock the chair over."

"Then why do you sound so scared?" Nog asked, his own voice getting edgy.

"Because it destroys living tissue," Jake said. "Think of a phaser set on highest power. When it hits a target, the target vanishes. The molecules just fly apart. Well, a vandellium bomb is like that, but all that flies apart is living tissue—flesh and bone and blood. Even a small vandellium bomb could destroy every living person within a five-kilometer area. They would all vanish in puffs of steam, along with all the animals and plants in the area."

"They're going to fly one of those up to Deep Space Nine," Sesana said.

Jake closed his eyes. He could feel his heart pounding. He imagined the *Einstein* docking at Deep Space Nine. Before Dr. Bashir could even go through the airlock, a small hidden bomb would explode with hardly a noise.

But Dr. Bashir would vanish—and Jadzia Dax, Keiko and Miles O'Brien, Quark, Major Kira, his own father if he had returned by then—and more than three hundred people aboard Deep Space Nine. Just momentary puffs of steam, and they would be gone. Then Deep Space Nine, intact and undamaged, would wait for the first to claim it. Jake had a feeling he knew who that first person would be.

Tikar Antol.

Haltingly, stammering a little, Jake tried to explain to the others just what a vandellium bomb could do to Deep Space Nine. "They need Dr. Bashir," he finished. "The shuttle security interlocks will only accept his ID patterns. And since he is expected, I don't think anyone on Deep Space Nine would give the shuttle a thorough scan before he docks."

"No," agreed Nog. "They can't. I overrode the circuits, remember? That's how we were going to get back undetected."

Jake almost groaned aloud. It wasn't just one Bajoran religious leader whose life was in peril. Everyone on Deep Space Nine was in danger. The three of them had to find some way to stop Tikar's plan.

But what could three kids do against Tikar Antol's army?

Jake did not know. Grimly, though, he realized that they would have to try.

CHAPTER 8

Jake studied the sketch that Sesana had drawn in the sand. "The prison hut is here," she said, touching a square with the tip of the rock she had used to mark the diagram. "There are two guards at the door. No windows."

Jake took a deep breath. The prison hut lay on the far side of the ravine, halfway up a gentle slope. Behind the hut were a couple of fuel tanks, and behind them was the sheer cliff face. There would be nowhere to hide once anyone got well inside the camp—and to get to the hut, the person would have to go right through the camp. It looked hopeless. Reluctantly Jake said, "I think we will have to ask for help, after all."

"Good!" Nog stood up and brushed the sand off his trousers. "Let's get started right away, and—"

"Not us, Nog," Jake said. He turned to Sesana. "You'll have to go back to town. Tell your father what's happening out here, and get him to notify the authorities. Maybe some of the monks will help—after all, Tikar is trying to assassinate the new Vedek, and—"

"I'm not going back," protested Sesana.

"You've got to," Jake insisted.

Sesana crossed her arms. "And what will you and Nog do while I'm gone?"

"We'll try to get the doctor out of camp," Jake said.

"Are you crazy?" asked Nog. "They have a whole army in there!"

"I know," Jake said. "But their army is half new, and almost untrained. And from what Sesana has told us, no one has found the rebel camp in years—they won't be expecting anyone to make a rescue attempt. I'll bet the guards are there just to keep Dr. Bashir from getting out, not to keep anyone else from getting in."

"You'll be taken on the spot," Sesana told them. "Tikar's army has no humans or Ferengi in it. I can get by, because I'm just another Bajoran face, but you—"

"Good point," said Nog. "Well, it's hopeless. Let's go."

"Hold on, Nog," Jake said. He was tired and grouchy. He stood up, feeling the coarse sand crunch beneath his feet. "Someone has to stay and try to rescue the doctor before they can drug him. If Tikar's going to let him die anyway when the vandellium bomb goes off, there's no telling what kind of drug they might give him. We have to try to get him out."

"Then let me stay and try to get to him," Sesana said. "You can go back and tell the authorities."

"That makes sense," said Nog. With a faint note of hope in his voice, he added, "Doesn't it make sense to you, Jake?"

"Sure," Jake said. "Only there's this one little matter. Nog, can you find your way back to Sakelo?"

"Of course!" Nog sounded indignant. "A Ferengi has an unerring sense of direction."

"All right," Jake said. "What direction is Sakelo City from here?"

Nog pointed.

Jake glanced at Sesana. She shook her head and pointed in an entirely different direction. Jake said, "There you are. You and I couldn't find our way back to the city—only Sesana can. So she has to go and we have to stay."

They argued some more, but in the end Sesana had to admit that Jake was right. She was the only one who could go back to the city for help. She left them, moving silently away in the gathering darkness of the short summer night. "I hate this," muttered Nog.

"I'm not crazy about it myself," Jake replied. "What we need is a plan."

"What we need is a diversion," Nog said.

Jake nodded. "That's a good idea."

"Of course it is. One of the Rules of Acquisition is that the greater amount you are taking from someone, the greater the distraction must be." Nog made a depressed clicking sound with his tongue. "I figure that we need a distraction about the size of a landquake. Any ideas?"

Jake had to admit he had none. They explored a little under the cover of darkness, and they found that they could climb the rockslide all the way up to the lip of the ravine here. The Turnaway camp had become a field of dark building and tent shapes dotted with the orange glows of cooking fires. It was a little startling to see just where the cloaking device cast its cover over the camp. One second Jake could see the fires clearly; when he took another step up the slope, half of them disappeared under the cloak. Another couple of steps, and they were all gone. Jake slipped, and a small rock clattered away under his feet.

"Quiet!" pleaded Nog. "They may have electronic ears out."

"Then they'd hear you for sure," Jake said with a grunt. The small stone rattled to a stop somewhere down the slope. An idea began to form in Jake's mind then. "Hey," he said, "I think you were right, Nog. The ideal diversion would be a landquake."

"Great," Nog said. "How do we start one? I'm not well acquainted with Federation techniques of destabilizing a planet's core."

"Not a real landquake," Jake said. "But a landslide. We can manage that with a few well-placed boulders."

Nog caught on immediately. "The rim of the Rip has lots of rocky spots where we could pry loose some big stones," he said. "If we sent two or three of those down, they might start an avalanche."

"At least they'd get the attention of everyone in the camp," Jake replied. "And small rockslides must happen often here. They might not even think someone started it."

"But they'd have to investigate," Nog said. "Because even a natural rockslide could destroy the camp, or part of it, anyway. Okay, let's go."

They climbed up to the edge of the Rip and carefully picked their way along the edge. Fortunately, the summer-glow lingered on the horizon, giving them enough light to see the likely spots. Jake found a place which had to be over part of the camp. It looked ideal.

Erosion had loosened a cluster of four or five large boulders there. The lower, larger ones were far too big for Jake and Nog to move, but the few on the top were smaller. If the boys could start them rolling, they would very likely knock loose at least a couple of the bigger stones, and once those started, an alarming rockslide would surely result.

For about an hour Jake and Nog labored over the most likely stone, chipping away at the pebbles and soil that held the boulder in place. Finally the rock was so loose that Nog could easily push it over the edge of the Rip. "You'll have to wait until I can get back down into the ravine," Jake said, panting. Using a rough stone as a chisel had blistered his hands, and his mouth was dry. "Give me about another hour, and then send the rock over."

"Go," said Nog in a weary voice. "I'll meet you at the top of the big rockslide—if we live long enough to meet."

The climb down was harder than the climb up, because the sky had grown darker and because Jake had to be careful to watch his step. It wouldn't do to slip and start a rockslide here—especially since Jake did not know how close any guards might be, or what sensors they might be using. Still, Jake reached the Rip floor in plenty of time. He stealthily picked his way across the jumble of stones at the bottom, getting as close as he dared to the entrance. Minutes crawled by. From here Jake could see the campfires again, and a breeze brought him the smell of burning wood and of cooking food. He could also hear faint voices, although they were so far away that he could not understand what they were saying.

After he had waited so long that he felt like an aching statue crouched behind a boulder, Jake was almost ready to believe that something had gone wrong. What if the Turnaways had patrols up on the edge of the Rip, and what if they had captured Nog? What if they knew already that he was out here, and what if they should send a squad armed with phasers to search for him? What if—

Crash! The sound of a huge rock bounding down the

side of the Rip somewhere up ahead yanked Jake out of his worried thoughts. Then, with a roar and a clatter, more stones fell. Jake heard shouts of alarm coming from the camp, and he set off at a trot, bending low and trying to keep boulders between him and any watchers. As he got closer, Jake could hear what the Turnaways were shouting: "Another fall—get away from the cliff!" and "We need some help over here, quick—one of the huts is blocked!" All the rest was confusion, shouts and curses and the hubbub of lots of people caught by surprise.

Jake finally came right up to the entrance. He could see now that the camp had a kind of dry moat around it, feeding into the central drainage channel. A metal drawbridge lay across it, but the guards fortunately had not drawn it up. Even better, the guards had apparently run to help the Turnaways who had been trapped in a hut by the slide. Jake hurried across it, hoping that no detection device was going off.

He blundered right into a couple of Bajorans who were carrying spades and pickaxes. "Watch it," one of them growled at him in the dark.

Jake ducked around to the rear of the first line of tents and huts. He closed his eyes and remembered where Sesana had said the prison hut was. It should be a little ahead of him, and off to the left, between two large cylindrical tanks. It was still very dark, but the cooking fires, near the central drainage channel, gave some light. Looking up, Jake could see the stars, but they wavered and danced in an odd way. He realized he was looking through the cloaking device that kept the camp safe. He only wished it gave a little illumination.

He came to the first tank, as big as a house and made of rusty metal. Jake flattened himself against it and crept around the curve. Yes, there was a hut ahead, and it was unguarded. He dashed to it and tried the door. It clanked, and he bent close to see a primitive padlock. "Who's there?" asked a sharp voice from inside. Jake recognized the speaker at once: Dr. Bashir.

"Me, Jake Sisko," he called back as loudly as he dared. "I'm going to get you out. Wait a second!"

Jake felt around in the dark. Large stones were plentiful, and he picked up one half the size of his own head. He pounded at the lock with this, making sparks fly. The first attempt was a failure, and Jake was almost afraid to try again—and then he heard the noise of another rockslide over across the way. He grinned. Nog was outdoing himself! In the resulting confusion Jake hammered away at the lock, sometimes hitting it, sometimes missing it, once skinning his finger badly. At last it gave way with a sharp *spang!* Jake shoved the door open.

Dr. Bashir, rumpled and unshaven, stood just inside, his face showing confusion in the wavering light of an antique oil lamp. "Jake!" he exclaimed. "How did you even find me? Who else has come?"

"Just Nog," Jake said. "Let's hurry—they may notice something's going on at any minute."

"Right," the doctor said.

They paused a moment in the doorway, and when the coast looked clear, both of them dashed out and through the night. Both Jake and Dr. Bashir stumbled and slipped, and once Jake ran right into the corner of a small hut that he could not see in the darkness. But somehow or other they made it all the way to the last tent. Just ahead lay the metal bridge—and coming across it was a group of six Bajorans, three of them carrying torches. Two of them held on to a struggling, writhing figure.

"Oh, no," said Jake with a groan. Their plan had succeeded, but only partially. Dr. Bashir was out of captivity—but now the Turnaways had captured Nog!

CHAPTER 9

If you want to be a hero," Jake whispered, "now is a good time."

Beside him Dr. Bashir crouched. They were behind a tent, and just on the other side a furious Tikar Antol was roaring orders. "This one says a friend of his is going to Sakelo City to bring back the authorities. You, Veldor! Take Beklesh with you and go in the fastest landtran to stop this friend. You can use the pheromone sensor to pick up the trail."

"What do we do with him?" a deep voice asked.

"Kill him and toss him into the Rip, for all I care," snarled Tikar. "Wait, though! Maybe you had better bring the friend here for questioning. Nothing must prevent the death of the Vedek tomorrow—we have to know whether the monks suspect that a real attempt will be made."

"Come on," Dr. Bashir whispered to Jake.

"But they have Nog—" Jake began.

"And I'm getting him back. Come with me—I know what I'm doing."

Jake followed as the doctor hurried away. The camp was slowly returning to normal after the hubbub and confusion of the rockslides, but no one challenged them. They came to a domed stone structure with a mesh steel gate at one side. Dr. Bashir groaned as he tested the gate and found it locked. "This is the garage," he explained hurriedly. "All the landtrans are in here. If we could get to them—" He stepped back and studied the building. "Look," he said. "There's a sort of ledge above the gate there. Do you think you could climb up to it?"

"I could try," Jake said, feeling uncertain. He had not had a lot of practice at climbing.

"Then let's see if we can get up there."

Dr. Bashir clambered up the gate. At the top he reached up, grabbed the edge of the overhang, and swung out. Jake caught his breath, but the doctor managed to pull himself up, painfully and slowly. "Come on!" he said in a loud, urgent whisper.

The mesh was large enough so that climbing up the gate was almost like climbing a very steep ladder. Jake got to the top, reached up, and nearly lost his balance. He felt Dr. Bashir's hand close on his wrist. "I'll help," the doctor said. "Ready? Go!"

Jake kicked away from the building and tried to chin himself on the ledge. He got his shoulders up but realized that was as far as he could go under his own power. Fortunately, Dr. Bashir grabbed him and gave him a tremendous tug, and Jake landed on the ledge out of breath and shaky. "What now?" he asked.

"Now we sit tight until they bring the landtran out," the doctor said. "We'll have to jump into it. It's about a six-foot drop, so we'll have to be careful. I'll take the driver, and you go for the passenger. And don't miss, whatever you do!"

With no trouble at all, Jake could think of about a dozen reasons not to follow the doctor's plan, but before he could mention any of them, two men came hurrying up to the garage. Jake saw them right under him as one of them unlocked the gate and rattled it open. "Both phasers on full charge?" that one asked the other man.

The other one, whose voice revealed him to be Veldor, said, "I've checked them both." He was carrying two short, rifle-shaped objects, phasers mounted to serve as medium-range personal weapons. The two men disappeared from view. A moment later Jake heard the whine of a landtran.

Dr. Bashir touched his arm. "They'll come out slowly," he said. "One will have to get out to lock the gate. When they first come through, we'll have to jump at the same time."

A yellow glare showed below, the headlamps of the landtran. It came nosing out of the garage. Dr. Bashir yelled, "Now!" and before he could take time to think about it, Jake leapt.

The landtran had seats for the driver and a passenger, but the rear of it was an empty, open bed, like an ancient Earth truck. Jake and the doctor landed there, hard, but even before the two passengers could yell, Dr. Bashir had snatched up one of the phasers. The unlucky Veldor had tossed them behind the driver's seat. "Out," Dr. Bashir said. He waved the phaser menacingly. "Jake, get the other weapon."

The leap had jarred Jake's recently injured ankle, and he gritted his teeth against the pain as he stooped to pick up the rifle. It was an unfamiliar device—Jake had never even fired a Federation phaser, and this one was bulky and heavy by comparison. Still, he held it the way that Dr. Bashir held his, hoping that he looked menacing.

Veldor, a hulking, bearded Bajoran, climbed out slowly. The other, Beklesh, was smaller and more obviously frightened. "Keep them covered, Jake," Dr. Bashir said. He moved into the driver's seat.

"You won't escape, human," said Veldor. "Tikar will have your head for this foolish attempt."

"Yes, well, compared to what he had in mind for me, that's rather a mild threat," replied the doctor. "All seems in order here. Veldor, give me the key to the gate. Now!"

The heavyset Bajoran cautiously produced the key and handed it over. "Into the garage, both of you," Dr. Bashir said. Over his shoulder he added, "Shoot them if they try anything. Full charge."

"Right," growled Jake, trying to make his voice sound deep and menacing. He hoped the two Bajorans wouldn't guess that he had no idea of how to fire this strange weapon.

As soon as the two were inside, Dr. Bashir slammed the mesh gate shut and locked it. Then he threw the key away into the darkness. He clambered back into the landtran and put it into motion. The land-car trundled down to a cleared strip running down the center of the camp, a strip that served as a rough street. "Now," said the doctor, "we have to rescue Nog. Jake, do you think you can drive this contraption?"

"I don't know," Jake confessed.

"Well, you'll have to try. Here, get behind the wheel."

Jake eased into the position. The "wheel" was actually shaped more like a figure 8 on its side. Dr. Bashir showed him how to accelerate by turning the right handgrip, and how to change gear speeds by turning the left one. "The brake is that pedal near your right foot," he said. "Now—straight out of the camp, and then turn around."

They were heading out the back of the camp, opposite from the side where Jake had entered. The landtran lurched and shuddered when Jake changed gears, but it rolled right along. "There," Dr. Bashir said. "Guardpost ahead. They'll be expecting Veldor to come through, and they'll expect him to stop. Don't."

"Okay," Jake said.

Two Bajorans were standing sentry duty here, far from Nog's rockslides of earlier that evening. They started forward casually, their phasers pointed down. The moment they seemed to realize that the landtran was not going to stop, one of them began to raise his weapon. Then Dr. Bashir suddenly stood up in the passenger seat and fired twice. Both guards dropped to the ground. "Don't worry," the doctor said as he dropped back into place. "I've set it on *stun.* They'll be all right in an hour or so. Watch the drainage ditch!"

They bumped along, the path becoming just the rubble-strewn floor of the Rip. "Stop for a second," the doctor said. "We have to think. It'll take at least an hour to get back to town, even at top speed—and that will mean leaving Nog behind."

"We can't just leave him," Jake said.

"No. But we're outnumbered, and at any second they

may swarm out after us. What do you think we should do, Jake?"

Jake felt miserable. How was he supposed to know? Adults were the ones who always wanted to take charge! He pulled himself together and said, "I don't think we have a choice. We have to go back for Nog."

"You're right. Turn around here," Dr. Bashir said after a few moments. "No, turn away from the ditch, not toward it. That's better." He sighed and added, "Well, at least we'll have surprise on our side. I'm surprised that we're doing this myself!"

Jake swung the landtran into a wide circle. He had to admit he was beginning to enjoy this. By comparison to the starship *Excalibur,* or even to the *Einstein* shuttlecraft, the landtran was a clunky, outdated piece of machinery, but to Jake it felt big and powerful. He took the last part of the circle slowly. "Now what?" he asked.

Beside him the doctor was clicking some control on the phaser. "Now," he said, "I want you to drive right through the center of the camp at top speed—and hope that the bridge is still down on the other side!"

"What are you going to do?" Jake asked, not able to keep some of his worry and fear out of his voice.

"I'm going to show up these Turnaways for what they are," said Dr. Bashir. Then he coughed self-consciously. "At least if I can shoot straight, I am. Be ready to brake if I tell you to. But then we have to pile right ahead as fast as possible. Veldor and Beklesh may have escaped from the garage by now, and we can't take chances. Ready? Go!"

Jake revved the engine to a splitting roar. The landtran

leapt ahead, its yellow headlamps picking out the way. Trying hard to keep the vehicle on a straight path, Jake followed his own treadmarks back into the camp. They whizzed past the stunned guards; then tents, metal huts, and fires were flashing past. Dr. Bashir pointed at a metallic dome in the very center of camp, off to their right. "There," he said. "That's my target. Hold it steady—"

The wind was blasting Jake's face. He squinted against it, and then he noticed that a gang of several men were running toward them, still far ahead. One of them had a hand phaser out and fired it, but the beam passed harmlessly by somewhere off to Jake's left. "They're shooting!" Jake yelled.

"Steady," the doctor said. "Here goes!"

He fired the phaser rifle. A white-hot beam of energy shot from it, blasted into the metal dome, and lit up everything around with an eerie blaze, like a bolt of lightning. The dome exploded with a red roar that flashed by to their right as they passed it. A split-second later, the shock wave hit, causing the landtran to lurch alarmingly. Ahead of them, the guards who had been running toward them staggered and fell, shielding their eyes. A second, deafening explosion went off behind them, and then the metal bridge was ahead. Now two sentries stood at it, but they leapt away as the landtran bore down on them, and neither was able to get off a shot.

Then they were out of the camp, into the round, sandy bowl where Jake, Nog, and Sesana had watched the Turnaways practicing and drilling. Jake headed for the

narrow space between the two rockslides. "All right," Dr. Bashir said. "I think you can stop and turn around now, but let's just wait here."

Jake was shaking from excitement, but he carefully stopped the vehicle, then jockeyed it around until it was turned back toward camp. He blinked. A fire was raging there, red flames and black smoke boiling up. "What did you do?" Jake asked.

"Tore the lid off the camp," the doctor replied. "You see, while he had me as his unwilling guest, Tikar Antol pointed out something that he was very proud of. It was a stolen Romulan cloaking device, and he had it in that metal dome. That's the only thing that lets the Turnaways stay here, you know—no one could detect them from the air, and no one on the ground knew quite how large the camp was or how much opposition they would face. Tikar said the people in town thought he probably had a couple of thousand soldiers here."

"And he didn't?" Jake asked.

"Maybe two hundred at the most," the doctor replied. "It's a big camp, but lots of it has been unoccupied since the Cardassians pulled out. Tikar has a fearsome reputation, but it's mostly based on bluff. Now the Bajorans will be able to see exactly how puny his threat is."

"Not to the Vedek, though," Jake said.

"That's true." The doctor's voice was thoughtful. "They have an assassin who will try to kill the new Vedek tomorrow at the installation ceremony. For me they had something a little more exotic planned, involving drugs and something even worse."

"I heard."

"Yes, well—" Suddenly Dr. Bashir stood up. "Here

comes Tikar," he said. "This is going to be the tricky part."

Jake swallowed hard. Whatever he thought of Tikar Antol, however ruthless and evil he seemed, there was no denying that the leader of the Turnaways was a brave man. With only two guards flanking him, he came striding out of camp, straight into the glare of the landtran's headlamps. He stopped a dozen paces away.

"Humans," he said, his voice oozing contempt. "I suppose you are proud of yourselves. You must think yourselves very clever indeed. But you forgot one small detail. We have that detail inside, and its name is Nog. If you surrender now, we will let the Ferengi live. If not—"

Casually Dr. Bashir leaned forward. "You are in no position to bargain, Antol," he said pleasantly. "We've delayed you too long now. Already the authorities in town know we're here, and that you held me prisoner. Already they have notified Deep Space Nine of that little fact. And, unfortunately for your plans, a Federation starship happens to be docked at Deep Space Nine. I don't think you're going to want to be here when the *Excalibur* shows up."

"You are lying," growled Tikar Antol.

"Believe that if you wish," Dr. Bashir said, his voice cool. "You will see the truth soon enough. Let me warn you, however, that the Federation does not treat its enemies with much mercy. Not when they kidnap officers and hold prisoner the son of a high Ferengi official, anyway."

Jake almost choked, but he managed not to laugh out loud at the doctor's description of Nog's father, Rom.

For a moment Tikar stood in the lights, his face rigid

with anger and frustration. Then he said, "What do you propose?"

Dr. Bashir waved his hand. "I don't think you'll be able to cloak your camp anymore. You'd best be on your way to find a new base. And I suggest when you leave, you'd do well to leave the vandellium device behind. We'll let the Starfleet weapons experts disarm it. You and your Turnaways have about five hours to travel as far from here as possible before dawn comes. Be sure you take everyone, Tikar—including your assassin. Otherwise, I can't be sure what my friends in Starfleet might do to you."

One of Tikar's henchmen began to protest, but Tikar cut him off with an angry glance. Then he stared at Dr. Bashir. "I have been a freedom fighter for a long time," he said. "I know when to take my losses and retreat. However, let me warn you that you have made a dangerous enemy of Tikar Antol. Our next meeting will not be so . . . pleasant."

"Send the Ferengi boy out," Dr. Bashir said. "Then you and your people can go anywhere you please. Just be away from this place by dawn, if you know what's best for you."

Tikar turned on his heel and walked back toward the camp. The fire was still leaping and sending up sparks from inside. After a moment Jake heard Dr. Bashir exhale.

"You were great," Jake said.

"I have never been so scared in my life," Dr. Bashir confessed in a trembling voice.

Startled, Jake looked at him. The doctor was sitting back in his seat, his eyes closed, his face glistening in the light of the distant fire. "I thought you wanted adventure," Jake said.

"I've had enough, thank you," returned the doctor.

Jake sat thinking about the Space Falcon and his latest triumph for a few minutes. Then a small figure came hurrying toward them. Jake grinned. It was Nog, safe and sound.

CHAPTER 10

If Sakelo City had seemed crowded when they first arrived, today it was absolutely bursting at the seams. Jake, Nog, and Sesana stared all around them at a huge, colorful throng of people, cheering, shouting, and waving.

A stately procession wound through the streets, a dozen wagons pulled by the strange green draft animals. The wagons wore decorations of flowers, red and orange, yellow and a startling blue-green, and in each wagon stood clusters of monks wearing equally brilliant robes.

Except for one flower-decked open carriage that held Jake, Nog, Sesana, Dr. Bashir—and the new Vedek. Sesana looked stunned. She had gone to her father the night before, and she had called out the city constables, all right. A force of them had met Jake and the others as they rode back toward town in the landtran. But then Sesana had found herself in deep trouble with her parents. Fortunately, Dr. Bashir had explained how vital her help had been, and then word had come from the

Vedek himself that all four were to join him in the procession.

Jake was still worried, for he remembered Tikar Antol's threat. Somewhere out in that crowd an assassin might still be lurking. Perhaps even now someone was aiming a phaser from a window, or preparing to toss a bomb, or—Jake swallowed. He did not like to think of all the murderous possibilities.

The procession stopped in one of the largest bazaars in the city, where a huge stage had been erected. The Vedek insisted on their accompanying him there. The grandfatherly old man strode to the center of the stage and lifted his hands for silence.

When at last the cheering had died down, he spoke. He said simple words, words that hoped for healing and for peace. Bajor was one world, he said, and no matter how much her children disagreed among themselves, they were still her children—one people, who had to realize their kinship and their duties to one another. Then he gestured to Dr. Bashir.

With a painful grin frozen on his face, the doctor walked forward. The crowd looked at him expectantly. Dr. Bashir cleared his throat and said, "Uh, as a citizen of the United Federation of Planets, I rejoice with you today. We wish for nothing more than the day when all Bajorans can live together in harmony and peace. It is a big universe, my friends. There is room in it for every belief—and room enough for every believer to respect all the others." Then he waved.

The people in the bazaar cheered him wildly, but when he turned away, the doctor still wore his sickly grin. "Now, that is frightening," he whispered to Jake.

"What? Did you see an assassin?" Jake asked.

The doctor shook his head. "No. I mean speaking in public," he muttered.

The ceremony went on for two more hours. Long before it was over, Sesana, Jake, and Nog managed to slip away. "Your friend has done the Bajoran Council a great favor by standing with Vedek Carik," she told them. "They will think more kindly of the Federation now."

"I hope so," Jake said. "All that worry and danger should be worth something."

"When do you leave for Deep Space Nine?" asked Sesana.

"In a few hours," Nog said. "Which means that I have no time for trading. Oh, well, my uncle can make some sort of profit from these trinkets." He rattled his backpack, which now held all sorts of trade goods.

Sesana smiled at him, and then she unfastened the chain that she wore around her neck. "Here," she said, handing the anthrolite necklace over. "This is the prettiest one I ever found. I hope it makes you happy."

Nog's eyes lighted up. "You are a beautiful and kind lady," he said. "If ever there is any service I can do for you, you have only to speak. I'll give you bargain rates."

Jake rolled his eyes. "I hope we can come back some day," he said. "Or maybe you can visit Deep Space Nine."

"I'd like that," Sesana confessed. "It must be beautiful to be out in space, away from all the dull cares and worries of a planet like Bajor."

With a smile Jake said, "Well, let's just say that living in space has its moments."

Jake, Nog, and Dr. Bashir left that afternoon on the *Einstein.* Nog was all curiosity. "Why didn't Tikar Antol try to kill the Vedek?" he asked. "In that crowd, anyone could have taken a shot at him."

"I know the reason," Jake told him. "It's because Dr. Bashir let Tikar Antol know that the *Excalibur* is in the neighborhood."

"Right," the doctor said, his voice surprisingly grim. "You see, the Turnaways have no place to hide now. If the Bajoran Council thought that he had assassinated a leader like the Vedek Carik in the presence of Federation representatives, they would surely invite Starfleet intervention. That's the last thing that Tikar would want—especially now that he no longer has that little vandellium bomb."

"They found it, then?" asked Nog.

"The constables brought it in. It's in a safe place now. The Council will ask Starfleet to disarm it."

Nog did not look as if he were reassured. "What if he gets another one?"

"I don't think that's likely. This one was stolen from a Cardassian force, years ago. Even the Cardassians rarely used them, though, so it's unlikely that any are left on the planet. And making one is out of the question, considering Bajor's level of technology."

Jake sighed. "I'd like to go back to Sakelo City some day," he said.

"So would I," Dr. Bashir said, his voice sarcastic. "But this time alone. Do you boys know how much trouble you're in?"

"What!" roared Nog. "You don't mean you're going to turn us in?"

"Nog, they must know by now that you've been away," Dr. Bashir replied. "They—"

"Listen," Nog said. "We have it all arranged. My father has seen to it that everyone thinks Jake is with me. With luck, we'll get back to Deep Space Nine and no one will be the wiser. Adults don't notice kids, except when they're in the way."

Dr. Bashir shook his head. "That's no good. I'll simply have to tell your parents what happened."

"Oh, man," groaned Jake. He doubted if he would ever see a planet again after his dad heard about this little stunt. And certainly not Bajor—not after Sakelo City had proved to be every bit as dangerous as Commander Sisko had feared. "Do you *have* to tell?"

"I can't see any way out of it," the doctor told them. "After all, I'm an adult, and I knew that the trip could be risky. You boys could have been killed, and then—"

"What!" Nog said. "Hey, we weren't the ones who went off with old Tikar and got captured."

Dr. Bashir frowned. "That's beside the point. You stowed away, and that's a serious offense."

"Wait a minute," Nog said. A crafty grin spread across his face. "Let's take a Ferengi approach. Maybe we can bargain a little about this. First, you'll admit we saved you."

"Well," Dr. Bashir said, "you helped, certainly, but as a matter of fact, I was planning my escape even before Jake showed up."

Nog gave Jake a meaningful look. "Right," he said. "But we did help."

"Yes-s," said Dr. Bashir slowly. "You did help."

"That's right," Jake said. "We were there when you needed us." Although he gave no sign of it, he felt a deep gratitude toward Nog. His Ferengi friend would not be in trouble, because Quark had plotted with Rom to get them down to the surface. Nog was doing all this for Jake's benefit—and at absolutely no charge. It was a wonderful act of friendship for a Ferengi.

Nog took up the argument: "And if we hadn't been, and if your own plan did not work, you would have been drugged, and the vandellium bomb would have wiped out everybody on Deep Space Nine, and all the crews of all the ships docked there, right?"

"Yes," said Dr. Bashir again. "What are you getting at, Nog?"

But Nog wasn't quite ready to tell. "And," he said, "if we hadn't helped, and your own plan had failed, then the new Vedek would have been killed. Maybe someone less friendly to the Federation would have taken his place. Correct?"

"I still don't see what you're trying to say," Dr. Bashir insisted.

"Simple," Nog replied. "If no one notices we have been gone, you just don't mention us at all. That way you get all the glory yourself. If people *have* noticed that we were away, then you tell them how much we helped you. If we helped you to escape and to save the Vedek's life, then we did a good thing. If we saved Deep Space Nine from a vandellium device, we did something even better. They can't be too hard on us for all that. Anyway, that would be lots better than the alternative."

"And what is the alternative?" asked Dr. Bashir suspiciously.

Nog looked at Jake. Jake grinned. "The alternative," he said, "would be that we tell everyone on Deep Space Nine how we went on a spy mission with the Space Falcon."

Dr. Bashir's tan face grew very red. "You—you heard that?" he asked.

"Every word," Nog said.

After a moment the doctor gave a deep sigh. "Very

well," he said. "I'll promise this much, at least: I'll stress how much you boys helped me if you forget the Space Falcon ever existed."

"It's a deal," said Nog.

Jake relaxed. In the viewscreen Deep Space Nine was visible in the distance, its strangely shaped bulk dark against the velvet blackness of space, but spangled over with lights. Jake watched it with mixed feelings. He had wanted some time on a planet, and he had managed to get some—even if it was not what he had expected. Now, though, he was returning to Deep Space Nine, and he felt a strange sort of comfort in the thought. He and his father were people of Earth, but now they lived out here, among the stars.

And Jake was going home.

About the Author

BRAD STRICKLAND has been writing science fiction and fantasy since 1982. He has published eight novels alone and two in collaboration with John Bellairs. He is the author of *Deep Space Nine:* #1 THE STAR GHOST. In everyday life, Brad teaches English at Gainesville College and lives in Oakwood, Georgia, with his wife, Barbara; their son, Jonathan; their daughter, Amy; a huge white rabbit; one small dog; one large dog; six cats; and an iguana. Although Brad is a big science fiction fan, he thinks that none of the inhabitants of his house are aliens, with the possible exception of two of the cats.

About the Illustrator

TODD CAMERON HAMILTON is a self-taught artist who has resided all his life in Chicago, Illinois. He has been a professional illustrator for the past ten years, specializing in fantasy, science fiction, and horror. His original works grace many private and corporate collections. He has co-authored two novels and several short stories. When not drawing, painting, or writing, his interests include metalsmithing, puppetry, and teaching.